Raven and the Ratcatcher

John Raven, retired from the Metropolitan C.I.D., is living in his barge *Albatross*, moored in the Thames in London. His latest troubles start when his sister rings to tell him her *au pair* girl has vanished; she expects Raven to do something about this.

Raven soon discovers the reason why the girl didn't answer her telephone: she is dead – the result of a botched abortion.

Raven reports to the police. At Chelsea police station he meets an enemy from the past, Commander Drake. These two have an old score to settle, and it looks as though the case of the dead girl will give them a chance to settle it.

The girl's death is not the simple tragedy it appears to be. Someone has planted a bag of gelignite in her flat. And the discovery puts Raven on the track of the very rough villain known as the Ratcatcher.

It is the duel between Raven, the lone-wolf, on the one hand, and the Ratcatcher and his fellow mobsters on the other, that provides the backbone of a thrilling plot. Raven's cold eye penetrates the seedy aspects of the City, its shabby wharves, docks and river, its squalid clubs, its oily gleaming streets through which crooks and police hunt each other in cars or on foot.

This is the third of Donald MacKenzie's novels in which John Raven has featured, and it may be that Raven is at his best, his adventures most exciting, amid this harsh portrayal of the London of today.

By the same author

RAVEN AND THE RATCATCHER

DONALD MacKENZIE

M

ISBN: 0 333 21162 6

First published 1977 by
MACMILLAN LONDON LIMITED
London and Basingstoke
Associated companies in New York
Dublin Melbourne Johannesburg and Delhi

Printed in Great Britain by
NORTHUMBERLAND PRESS LIMITED
Gateshead

$\frac{F}{8}$
598991

For
Christopher Radmall

Guns aren't lawful
Nooses give
Gas smells awful
You might as well live.

Dorothy Parker

CHAPTER ONE

It was November and London was wet, cold and miserable. The rain had been falling since early morning, pitting the surface of the swollen river. I was still in pyjamas, listening to records. I live on a converted barge I call the *Albatross*. In the ten years that I've owned her, she hasn't shifted more than a couple of feet in her moorings. The previous owner had the barge ballasted with scrap iron and caulked by a naval pensioner. There are many houseboats moored in Chelsea Reach that are more elegant, few that are more comfortable.

I have two bedrooms, my own and a rarely-used guest room. There's a large sitting room, a decent kitchen with a freezer and dishwasher, a bathroom, telephone and mains electricity. Most of the furniture is either Georgian or Victorian, stuff from the old house in Suffolk, pieces that Cathy and I picked up together at sales. Offhand, I can't think of anywhere that I'd prefer to live.

The oil-heaters generated an acrid fug and I was lying on my back on the sofa, enjoying Chopin. The phone rang. I took off the cans and dragged the phone across the floor by the cord. It had to be my sister. No one calls me any more at three-thirty in the afternoon. A V2 rocket orphaned the pair of us in 1944 and Anne has been trying to organise my life ever since. She's married to a lecturer at the London School of

9

Economics, a man called Jerzy Urbanovic, friend of the oppressed and dedicated left wing sympathiser. It's a matter of record that as a child Jerzy was dragged across Europe, from Warsaw to Budapest to Cairo and Jerusalem. For the next five years most of his education came at the hands of regimental drivers and Arab maid-servants. Colonel and Mme Urbanovic seem to have been less concerned with their son than with gracious living. In any case, the war over, Jerzy landed in England, twelve years old and with a hatred of everything Polish and aristocratic. He must have had brains, running a scholarship into a First in Economics and becoming a lecturer before he was thirty-five. He's a good husband and father and I've always loathed the sight of him. It isn't only the radical chic. I can ignore the pipe-smoker poses, the instructions about 'the dictatorship of the proletariat'. What I cannot ignore is his tacit approval whenever Anne chooses to criticise my morals or eating habits. He neither agrees nor disagrees openly, seeming to rise above it all by some feat of moral levitation that makes me want to ram his head down through his knees.

'Yes,' I said, trying to lock the wariness out of my voice.

'What are you up to?' Anne demanded promptly.

I hesitated. According to her, a man of thirty-nine is supposed to find better things to do with his time than enjoy himself. Something in the nature of self-redemption, for instance. I am the first in the family to choose a career as a cop. Anne manages to combine relief at my premature resignation with a suspicion that I must somehow have disgraced myself.

'Nothing much,' I said. 'You know, letters and things.'

'I'm worried,' she answered.

'What about?' I put the question guardedly, thinking that it might have had something to do with the children. There are two of them, a boy and a girl. Basha is freckled and button-nosed while Tomek takes after his father. At the age of eight he offered to teach me how to play chess. The trouble was that he was fully capable of doing so.

I made a show of avuncular interest. 'Are the kids all right?'

'They're in good form,' she said quickly. 'It's Olga.'

I tried to fit a face to the name and failed. 'Olga?' I repeated.

Her voice sharpened. 'Don't be so bloody vague, John. The *au pair*. God knows you spent enough time looking at her legs.'

I seldom go to Hampstead. The house is usually full of freethinkers quoting Regis Debray and eating processed cheese and limp dill-pickles.

'Are you listening to me?' she demanded.

'What else,' I said resignedly. The arm lifted on the turntable, leaving me with the sound of the rain and creaking timbers. The room was warm and comfortable and she was going to get me out of it. I knew this instinctively.

Her voice drilled into my ear. 'I told you that she left here. That must have been six months or so ago, to share a flat with some other girl. I'm not going to pretend that I was too happy with the idea. After all, I am responsible to her parents.' I held the receiver away from my ear, watching the gulls wheel outside the windows. 'And in any case girls of that age are far more independently-minded than we were.'

'Crap,' I replied.

'*What* did you say?' she demanded.

'I said a wholly unlikely statement.'

Anne sniffed. 'Anyway this flat was somewhere in South Kensington. Clare Street. She was still coming to work here, of course, and as far as I know attending her evening classes. On Tuesday she called to say that she had the 'flu. Headache and running a temperature. I told her to stay in bed and call the doctor. Then this morning someone telephoned from the Aliens Office, asking for Olga. The man said it was a routine inquiry, something to do with the renewal of her visitor's permit. Are you paying any attention at all to what I'm saying?'

'What do you want?' I retorted reasonably. 'Oohs and aahs?'

She sniffed again. 'The thing is, Olga doesn't seem to have reported her change of address. The man made this perfectly clear. They still think that she's living with us.'

I tucked my bare feet deep under the cushions. 'And you told him she wasn't.'

'I did nothing of the sort,' she replied calmly. 'She's a good girl and the children adore her. The last thing I want is to get her into trouble.'

Anne concerns herself with other people's children who are left in cars, the Race Relations Act and the plight of distressed gentlefolk. Her drive and interest are not always appreciated.

I slid down further on my shoulders. 'Then you're being stupid. She's a Swiss subject, an alien and you sponsored her entry into the country. The law says that she's supposed to report any change of address, any stay of more than twenty-four hours away from her registered address. What kind of excuse does she give?'

'That's the whole point. I just don't know. I've been ringing her flat all day but nobody answers.'

'And you want me to do something about it,' I said resignedly.

'Well you know how Jerzy is. Anything to do with the law.'

I knew. As a man whose father was refused British citizenship, Urbanovic slavishly obeys all directions by vested authority, including KEEP OFF THE GRASS signs. I could see that it wouldn't please him to hear that his *au pair* was flouting the very regulations he himself respected so deeply.

'I have to talk to you about it,' Anne continued. 'Before Jerzy gets home.'

I can remember a games-master at one of my prep schools using a slipper on me to reinforce the dictum that life is full of compromise. But I've never believed in doing things that I don't want to do if it can be avoided. This seemed to be one occasion when I was well and truly hooked.

'O.K.,' I said wearily. 'Where?'

She gave me the name of a department store in Finchley. The restaurant up on the fourth floor served afternoon teas. We arranged to meet there as soon as I could make it. I shaved, found some cords and a turtleneck sweater. I topped these with my poncho and opened the door leading out on deck. The wind blew rain in my face. I gave up wearing hats seven years ago when I started growing my hair long. Rain, I thought, wet, walking, Mrs Burrows. I went back to the kitchen and left a note for her.

Bacon, eggs and sugar, please! And get the apple-cores from under the bed!!

Exclamation marks impress Mrs Burrows. She's sixty-seven years old and has been with me for eight of them. She refuses to accept my retirement, having taken it into her head that I'm still on the force, seconded to some kind of super-sleuth activity that allows me to keep an eye on the goings-on along the Embankment. People tell me that she's not above warning neighbours to watch their step. She has her own keys and comes to me on Mondays, Wednesdays and Fridays.

There's a door at the end of the gangway that's cemented into the stonework of the Embankment. With the exception of *Albatross* the fourteen houseboats in the moorings are connected by a network of ropes and planks. It makes things easy for the local boy-burglars who rip off anything that isn't screwed down. So I've put barbed wire across the top and around the sides of the gangway entrance. The rain was falling in stair rods, making the planks greasy.

The street lamps were already lit, goldfish bowls strung along the sides of the river. I waited for a lull in the traffic, water trickling down my neck. A break came and I sprinted for my car. I've driven a Citroën ever since I left the force. With legs as long as mine it's difficult to achieve a comfortable driving-position. I set the windshield-wipers working, thinking of the inconsistencies in Anne's sense of values. She and her husband were on the mailing list of every crank organisation in the country yet she seemed to be quite happy exploiting a foreign student. Anne's *au pairs* earned less than I paid Mrs Burrows.

The Country Fare is a store that is Hampstead's

answer to Harrods, a highrise building of black glass, Italian ceramics and trees growing up on the roof. I left my car in the subterranean garage and took the lift to the fourth floor. It was years since I'd seen the like. A three-piece string orchestra of middle-aged ladies dressed in woollen knitwear was playing *Pale Hands I Loved* to an indifferent audience of Finchley Road matrons. Anne was sitting at a table near the entrance. There was a pot of tea in front of her. She never eats between meals.

I touched her cheek with my lips. I've always shied from kissing women on the mouth, even my sister. It's been suggested that I hated my mother but since I never knew her I doubt it. I dropped into the chair opposite Anne. Something must have gone wrong with the genes in our family. I'm six feet three inches tall and according to the charts about fifty pounds underweight. Anne is a foot shorter and weighs about the same as I do. She'd had diet problems since Basha was born. She's taken to wearing dirndls and peasant-blouses and with her yellow plaits she looks like Trudi in some Alpine operetta.

She terminated her inspection with a shake of her head. 'I thought men were wearing their hair longer these days.'

It was the sort of remark that bags two birds with one barrel. My hair was both too long and unfashionable. She filled my cup from the tea pot. It was China tea and lukewarm. I looked over my shoulder, smiled and crooked a finger at the waitress. She detached herself from the wall and swivel-hipped to our table.

'I'd like some toast, please. Indian tea and milk.'

15

She scribbled the order and lodged the pencil in her beehive hairdo.

'We usually do serve milk with Indian tea, sir.'

Anne waited till the woman was out of earshot. 'I love it when you're put in your place. You look so bewildered.'

I lit a cigarette. Anne's one of those people who exude wholesomeness. There's a suggestion of lavender-sachets hanging in wardrobes, of stoneground flour and windows thrown wide open. The truth is that I remember her as an eager virgin with immodest intentions towards my schoolfriends.

'Let's get down to the nitty-gritty,' I said.

She made a face as I gave her a light. 'What a revolting expression.' She smokes the brand advertised as having the lowest tar content. My cigarettes are French and lethal.

I knew that they were a reminder to her of Cathy. Anne never really liked the girl I lived with. The fact that she's dead doesn't seem to matter. Anne still resents her memory.

She lifted an enormous alligator bag from the floor beside her. I knew it of old. It bulges with fat diaries, old theatre-programmes, Milner's strong mint comforters, half-finished crochet-work and bunches of keys. She rummaged among all this and came up with a letter.

It was dated the previous October and written in formal English from an address in Montreux. M and Mme Suchard thanked Mme Urbanovic for her continued interest in their daughter and expressed their gratitude that she was in such good hands. I returned the letter to its envelope and gave it back to

Anne. The toast the waitress had brought was inedible.

'I remember. They came to London to see you before the girl arrived, didn't they?'

She blew twin streams of smoke, daringly. 'Yes they did. They're that sort of person. Very Swiss, very correct and very conscientious. On top of that Olga's their only daughter and they're completely devoted to her.'

My yawn was compulsive. The restaurant was over-heated and I found the subject less than enthralling.

'I still can't remember what she looks like. I'm confusing her with that Swedish girl.'

Anne produced a coloured snapshot showing a girl in her early twenties with reddish blonde hair. She was holding my sister's beagle hound in her lap and staring into the camera with solemn green eyes. Her legs were out of focus.

'I remember,' I said. 'The one who made watercress soup.'

'She's a really nice girl,' Anne replied.

'Aren't they all?' She's convinced that she's a superb judge of character. 'Remember the Persian princess who took off with your Henry Marks Fun Fur manteau?'

'That's different,' she said, sidestepping the reminder. 'I'm very worried about her, John. I certainly don't want to get her into any sort of trouble but somebody has to talk to her.'

She pushed a piece of paper across the table. There were two addresses written on it, a language-school near Queen's Gate and ninety-eight Clare Street, S.W.7.

'By "somebody" you mean me?'

Anne nodded. 'She'll listen to you.'

'And just what am I supposed to say to her?'

She gave me her mother-earth look. 'What I'd really

17

like, of course, is for her to come back and live at the house. It would be so much more suitable all round.'

I stuffed the piece of paper in my pocket. 'Suitable for you, possibly. I'm not so sure about her.' I signalled for the bill.

Anne slapped powder on her nose and pulled a beret low on her forehead.

'Don't be ridiculous! I'm responsible to her parents, remember.'

I shook my head firmly. 'Exactly. And if you're counting on me leaning on the girl, forget it. You'd probably lose her in any case. Why the hell *wouldn't* she prefer living with a friend? I know I would. The only mistake she made was not telling the people at the Aliens Office that she'd changed her address.'

The waitress appeared with the bill. I added a tip to the total. 'I suggest using blotting paper on that toast before you bring it out again.'

She pocketed the cash, giving me the sort of smile that waitresses reserve for awkward customers.

'Any particular colour, sir?'

Anne snapped her bag shut as the waitress walked away. 'You're rude and your face is red. Give me a ring as soon as you've talked to Olga. And remember, Jerzy's not to know a word of any of this.'

'I'll remember,' I promised, bending into the familiar smell of Mary Chess Jonquil than which, as Cathy used to say, nothing is more familiar.

CHAPTER TWO

It was still raining when I drove up the ramp. I turned right and headed for Maida Vale, into sodden avenues lined with desolate trees. Past redbrick blocks of flats where stockbrokers once kept chorus-girls, past Edwardian houses with squatter communes, dripping ivy, tap-dancing schools and kosher butchers staffed by fat men in white coats wearing straw hats. Hyde Park was sad with great stretches of deserted turf, the rabbits deep in their lakeside burrows and only the ducks on the stippled water.

Clare Street is between South Kensington Station and Fulham Road. I stopped outside the Underground and used the phone in the booking hall. Her number didn't answer. I drove south towards her address. Clare Street turned out to be a short row of Georgian houses with iron railings protecting basement areas.

The houses had been converted to flats, two floors up and two floors down. The front doors were painted in different colours. I parked opposite ninety-eight and switched off the motor. The windows of the lower flat were curtained in dingy nylon net. The two top storeys were sealed by white shutters, offering blank faces to passers-by. Lights were burning in the neighbouring houses but as far as I could see ninety-eight was in total darkness.

I crossed the street to the red door. A tub with a

drowned hydrangea in it was chained to the railings. There were two bell-pushes, one above the other. The metal frames for name-cards were empty. I put my thumb on the top bell and heard it ring upstairs. Water gurgled in the guttering as I waited for someone to answer. I tried again, without response, then used the lower bell. This time I couldn't even hear a ring. I lifted the letterbox flap and peeked through into the hallway. There was enough back-light from the street lamp to make out the travel posters hanging on the walls, the short flight of blue-carpeted stairs beyond. At the head of the stairs was a closed white door. I put my ear where my eye had been and heard a sound in the upper part of the house. It was difficult to be sure but the noise was like a cistern being flushed.

I left the car where it was and walked round into Clare Mews. Wet cobblestones glistened under the lamplight. A door in the row of lock-up garages was unlocked. I slipped through into a concrete yard with refuse bins scattered between the fire escapes. I walked along to the fourth house from the end. There was a gap in the basement net curtains. I could see bare floorboards, an empty kitchen and passage. The bottom flat was clearly unoccupied. I climbed the fire escape to the second storey. Olga Suchard's back door was panelled with frosted glass but I managed to peek through the red-checked curtains in a side-window. An ironing board leaned against the wall of a spotless kitchen. There were underclothes and a bowl of fruit on the table. An alarm clock on a shelf nearby showed twenty minutes to six.

I tapped on the frosted glass. Lights from a television screen flicked across the next fire escape. I heard the time signal for the evening news, the announcer's voice. I used my toe on the bottom of the door but nobody answered. I retreated down the iron stairs wishing that I'd had the wit to ignore Anne's phone call. I was at the door leading out into the mews when something made me look round. The rain was driving across my vision but for a second I thought I saw a face at Olga Suchard's kitchen window. When I looked again it was gone.

I drove north up Queen's Gate, stopping on the corner of Harrington Gardens. It's an area of Arab-owned hotels, private day schools and oddly-named restaurants. I pulled in behind a green M.G.B. A sign outside the porch of the house opposite read

THE COSMOS COLLEGE OF ADVANCED ENGLISH

(Proprietor Sebastian O'Toole)

I walked up the steps into a marble-floored hallway crowded with students who appeared to be waiting for classes to start. They were in their early twenties and of all shades of colour, chatting animatedly in English of varied accents. I made my way to the back of the hall where damp coats and umbrellas were hanging on hooks. The door to a classroom was half-open. Powerful lamps suspended from the ceiling shone on rows of empty desks. There was a strong smell of stale tobacco smoke. A man writing on a blackboard spoke without bothering to turn his head.

'Yes, what is it?'

I walked a few steps nearer. 'Mr O'Toole?'

He swung around to consider me with pale blue eyes set in a lowering face as white as the chalk in his fingers. He was wearing schoolmasters' uniform, corrugated grey flannel trousers and a tweed jacket leather-patched at the elbows.

21

'Do I *look* like Mr O'Toole?' he demanded.

'I wouldn't know,' I said reasonably. 'I've never seen him.'

He had the frustrated air of a man whose best has never been good enough and who knows it. He enunciated his words very clearly as if talking to a foreigner or an idiot.

'I am *not* Mr O'Toole. If it's about enrolling for classes, wait in the hall. The Principal will be in his office in about twenty minutes. More or less.'

His breath was a souvenir of his lunchtime drinking. 'It's not about classes,' I explained. 'I'm looking for one of your pupils, a Swiss girl.'

He put the piece of chalk down and wiped his fingers fastidiously. 'And does she have a name, this Swiss girl? There are approximately one hundred and twenty pupils enrolled. Unfortunately over half of them are women.'

'Olga Suchard,' I said.

It was obvious that the name meant nothing to him. He opened a register on his desk and consulted it.

'Miss Bullivant's class, Room Five. English Culture Studies.' The sarcasm was even plainer.

I kept my tone polite. 'You don't happen to know if Miss Bullivant is in the building?'

He shut his eyes, affecting to think. 'If Miss Bullivant were in the building it would greatly surprise me. I'll content myself with saying that when Mr O'Toole graces us with his arrival, Miss Bullivant will not be far behind.'

I thanked him and went back to the hall. I tried Olga Suchard's name on a group of Near East youngsters. Shrugs and blank stares answered me. There was a bulletin-board hanging on the wall. The notices displayed referred to various student activities, boat-trips to Greenwich, cheap tickets for the Old Vic.

I found the name Suchard on a list of people wanting to take Yoga lessons. Someone had scored the name out with a pencil. The voice behind me was warm and low pitched.

'Excuse me, please. Are you looking for Olga Suchard?'

I turned sharply. This girl was nothing like the one I had seen in the photograph. Her skin was faintly sunburned, her nose thin and straight, her dark eyes smiling. She was wearing a long black skirt, elegant boots and a heavy gold cross hanging over a ruffled silk shirt.

'My name is Teresa Cintron. I am Olga's friend.'

She was possibly twenty-two or three with an air of sophistication that set her apart from the other students. I introduced myself.

'If Olga's your friend, you've probably heard her speak of my sister Anne. Olga works for her.'

Her smile held. 'Of course. Olga speaks of her often. And the children.'

'Are you the girl she's sharing a flat with?' I asked.

'No,' she said slowly. She shook back shoulder-length hair, her eyes suddenly anxious. 'Is something the matter?'

'That's what I'm trying to find out,' I said. 'You see, she doesn't answer her phone and she's not at Clare Street. I've just come from there.'

We were still standing near the bulletin-board with an overhead light shining directly on her face.

She clasped her hands in an attitude of contrition. 'How stupid of me! You see, it is all my fault!'

She took the cigarette I offered, holding her hair back as I held out my lighter.

'How do you mean, your fault?' I inquired.

She blew smoke, smiling again. 'You know she's been sick? Well, I was there last night – I mean at Clare Street. Olga was feeling much better. She told me that a friend had asked her down to the country for a couple of days to rest. It all happened so suddenly. This girl arrived while I was there. She was going to drive Olga down to Berkshire. I was supposed to call your sister and explain. I completely forgot. What can I say?'

A bell rang and there was a general rush in the direction of the classrooms.

'Don't worry about it,' I said. She was plainly anxious to go. 'I'll explain to Anne what has happened. Tell Olga to get in touch as soon as she's back in London. It's reasonably important.'

By the time I'd reached my car I'd decided that Teresa Cintron was lying for some reason or other. Her story was too pat. The sudden recovery and forgotten phone call. My own feeling was that a man was at the back of it all. Teresa was probably doing a snow-job for a friend. In any case I'd done my brotherly duty and with luck would hear no more of Miss Olga Suchard.

A bus passed, showering the pavement with dirty water. Rainwashed windows blurred the faces of the passengers. It was rush hour and I took the short way home, down Drayton Gardens, across Fulham Road, and into Chelsea. Traffic lights held me at the junction of Kings Road and Oakley Street. I glanced left casually. People were waiting at the bus-stop, huddled under umbrellas. The reflection of a car showed in the shop window behind them. I looked up into the rearview mirror. It was the bottlegreen M.G.B. I'd seen parked outside the Cosmos School of Advanced English.

The lights changed. I accelerated down Oakley Street, the M.G.B. following me. The make and the colour were fairly common but I'd been mistrusting coincidences for almost nineteen years. The lights were with me as I came to the bridge. I turned left instead of going right towards home, gunned along the Embankment and stopped in front of Hamilton Court. I knew the block of flats facing the river. My lawyer lives on the fifth floor. I was up the steps in seconds and into the quiet warmth of the lobby. Strips of burlap had been laid to protect the carpet against muddy footsteps. The porter at the desk lifted his nose from his newspaper, offering a smile as he recognised me.

'A dirty evening, Mr Raven.'

'Terrible.' I nodded back towards the Embankment. 'I've left my car outside for a few minutes. There's no room opposite the pub.'

He showed me his thumb and returned to his newspaper. I walked along the corridor and left the building by a side-entrance. The pub across the street was an oasis in the misery of the evening, with gleaming brass and a coal fire. I took my drink to the window. There was a clear view east along the Embankment. The M.G.B. was parked outside Hamilton Court near my car. Teresa Cintron was in the driver's seat, watching the steps leading up to the lighted hallway. A cab arrived. The porter hurried out with a large umbrella, protecting the passenger from the rain. The windscreen wipers started to swish on the M.G.B., signifying that the motor had been restarted. The driver waited for a while as if committing the scene to memory, made a quick prohibited U-turn and vanished in the direction from which she had come.

I finished my drink and drove down to Chelsea Reach. I parked in the alleyway at the side of the Fourth Dimension Herborium and walked back. The lights were still on in the store. Worried-looking tropical fish were darting about behind a forest of thyme, bay and rosemary leaves stuffed into the window. A neighbour of mine owns the place, a man as tall as I am who wears granny glasses, jeans tucked into Spanish riding boots and dyes his hair green and his beard ginger. He lives with a Great Dane called Marmalade and gossip has it that the odd consignment of grass comes in with his herbs. So be it. He's a quiet neighbour and gives me parking privileges.

Albatross was wallowing a little on the rising tide, straining against the heavy-duty tyres that serve as fenders. There was the usual smell of cat-shit at the end of the gangway. The culprit lives three boats away, a ragged-eared tom who has survived three direct hits with my BB shot Daisy air-rifle. Mrs Burrows had been and gone, leaving the groceries on the table together with my change. She and I have a good relationship. She cleans the houseboat the way I like it, leaves my things alone and asks few questions. I pay her top rates and listen to bulletins on the state of her rheumatism. The sitting room had been vacuumed. The pile of records was still on the floor. My collection is one of my pleasures. I have more than seven hundred records, most of them classical music. It has nothing to do with cultural pretensions. Somebody happened to have had the good sense to play Bach to me as a child.

I put the eggs and the bacon in the refrigerator,

turned up the oil-heaters. People complain about the smell but to me it's part of home like the smell of the mud at low tide. My trousers were wet so I slipped them off and sat on the side of the bed. I've lived alone since Cathy's suicide. I suppose you could say that as far as women are concerned, I've realised my limitations. It's made me the object of a number of accusations. Conceit, cruelty, insensitivity. Women have called me a philanderer, a latent homosexual, but the truth is simple. I'm too selfish to share my life with anyone else. The situation has its drawbacks. For instance at Christmas I go to bed for three days. But by and large I manage to do things my own way. Money hasn't been a problem since Atlas Holdings took over the family business from the trustees. I never touched my salary the whole time I was on the force. I have the odd hassle with the accountants but there's always enough cash to meet my needs. I'm lucky. I have a Paul Klee and *Albatross*. I've never really wanted much more. Not in material terms, anyway.

I pulled on a pair of dry trousers and went into the sitting room. There are windows on both port and starboard sides, six walnut chairs, a table that came from Suffolk, a bronze horse I bought in Spain. My Klee is a splash of blue and black dominating the wall above the old torn leather sofa. An ex-con made my record-shelves, an old lag who'd spent most of his life in jail. I'd been the last one to nick him. He was seventy-four years old when he came out and for some reason brought his problems to me. It seems that way back he had learned some carpentry and I needed the shelves. He built them, died and was buried in a cemetery in South Wimbledon, completely forgotten. But the shelves held up which is as good a memorial as any, I suppose.

I put *Les Francs Juges* on the record-player and propped myself on the sofa, thinking about Teresa Cintron. Something about her voice and manner gave me the impression that she was South American. The idea that she was deliberately lying I found distasteful. It was probably no more than one girl covering up for another.

It was possible that Olga had a man living with her. Whatever the answer was, one thing was clear. My appearance at the language school had been panic stations for Teresa. It was important enough for her to cut class and follow me, either to know where I went or to follow me home. The more I thought about it, the less I believed in this tale that Olga was somewhere in Berkshire.

I lifted the phone on impulse and dialled the Clare Street number. Surprise, surprise. A girl's voice answered in a foreigner's English.

'Hello, yes?'

Her voice came quickly as if she'd been expecting the call. I gave her no time for reflection.

'Is this Olga Suchard?'

Her tone lost some of its eagerness. 'Yes. Who is it speaking, please?'

'John Raven, Anne's brother. We met at the house in the summer.'

'Of course,' she said slowly. 'Yes, of course, I remember.'

'Don't you think that you and I ought to have a chat?' I suggested.

'A chat?' She sounded frankly worried now. 'I don't understand, Mr Raven.'

'Then I'll explain. Someone from the Aliens Office has been ringing my sister's house and asking for you. It's something to do with renewing your visitor's permit. Didn't you know that you're supposed to notify any change of address?'

She sounded both contrite and worried. 'I did, of course. But I kept putting it off. I'm so sorry, Mr Raven. I shall send them a letter tonight, I promise.'

'I thought you were supposed to be in bed with the 'flu,' I suggested. 'Anne's been trying to get hold of you all day.'

'I was sleeping,' she said very quickly. 'I took some pills.'

'You didn't know you were supposed to be down in the country?'

'I'm sorry,' she replied. 'In the country? I don't understand.'

There was something definitely wrong about her manner though it was obvious that the Berkshire story wasn't hers. She might have had a man in the bed beside her but her morals were none of my concern.

'Call Anne anyway,' I said. 'She's worried about you.'

'I really am sorry.' She hurried the words, anxious to get me off the line. 'Goodnight, Mr Raven.'

She hung up, leaving me uncertain about calling my sister. The girl had sounded close to tears. The trouble was that my brother-in-law would be home by now. The simplest thing was for me to see for myself. I collected my car keys and poncho.

My last eight years on the force were spent at Scotland Yard, half of them working out of the Serious Crimes Squad. The experience taught me a number of things about myself. A policeman tends to interpret the law as well as enforce it. The pace and pressure of his occupation warp his thinking. It may seem an odd thing to say but few cops in the detective branch are happy. A detective by definition is a lonely man, never wholly accepted by the society he protects, often a stranger to his own family and forced into brief, unnatural acquaintanceships. The moment a cop starts wearing his own clothes on duty, values change. He even begins to *look* different, furtive-eyed, dressing and talking like the villains he hunts. The once familiar becomes an object of suspicion and justice matters less than expediency. There's little room for compassion. The machine is inexorable. If I hadn't resigned I'd probably have gone the way of the others. As it is, I'm still capable of feeling embarrassed. If a hostile young man answered Olga Suchard's doorbell I'd understand his feelings.

I put some money in my pocket. It was seven o'clock and the rain was still pelting down. A few cars were parked outside the pub across the street. I avoid the place on principle. It's recently been discovered by a coterie of self-confessed geniuses. Writers who never write, garlic-breathed painters with political revelations and androgynous television producers.

The Citroën subsided under my weight, locking me comfortably behind the steering wheel. I drove north to Clare Street and found a slot to park near the red-painted front door. The shutters upstairs were still closed but the light was on in the hallway.

I tapped a smoke from the packet and lit it. There was a chance that Olga might have called Anne by now, having sent off the letter to the Aliens Office notifying her change of address. If this turned out to be true, my arrival on her doorstep could justly be described as poking my nose into someone else's business.

Footsteps were coming along the street. I wound down my window. A man's reflection grew in the rearview mirror, a short man walking quickly with an umbrella held in front of his face. He passed the line of parked cars, hesitated as he neared number ninety-eight then turned and came back. I saw him clearly as he passed beneath the street lamp, neat anonymous clothes with a neat anonymous face. He was carrying what looked like a gladstone bag. He walked to the end of the street then retraced his steps. This time he stopped and rang Olga Suchard's doorbell. The front door opened immediately. The angle made it impossible for me to see into the hallway. The visitor stepped inside, wiped his feet and the door closed again. I pitched my cigarette through the open window, watching it spiral through the rain and drown in the gutter. I felt as an actor must, finding himself onstage with the wrong cue. The visitor might have been anyone, friend, relative, even lover. Women's choice of men no longer surprises me nor for that matter vice-versa. One thing was sure. Whoever he was, the stranger had been expected.

A fresh downpour drummed on the roof of the car, the rain splashing my face. I wound up the window and switched on the radio. A Beethoven symphony was playing and for a while I was indifferent to everything but the music. I've no idea how much time passed, we were well into the Choral, when the red door burst open. The stranger emerged, slamming the door behind him with such force that the lock failed to catch. I could see the posters in the hallway fluttering in the sudden current of air. The man looked left and right, struggling all the while to get his umbrella up, his bag clutched under an arm. By the time he reached the corner he was running. Seconds later I heard the unmistakable noise of a Volkswagen moving away at speed.

The lamp in the hallway laid a strip of yellow light through the partly-open door. I crossed the street and stood by the hydrangea-tub, listening. All I could hear was the gurgle of water in the guttering. I pushed the door open and called. There was no answer. The entrance to the bottom flat was on my left, the stairs leading to the upper part of the house straight ahead. Olga's white door was wide open. I closed the street door behind me and went up the stairs. Chrysanthemums were growing on a window ledge on the half-landing. A second flight of stairs and I was standing outside the darkened kitchen. A pedestal-lamp was burning next door in the sitting room. A cheroot-end was smouldering in an ashtray. There must have been a thousand flats like it in the neighbourhood, furnished with the gleanings of attic and storeroom and rented at exorbitant rates. The sofa and chairs were covered with faded chintz, Aubrey Beardsley prints hung on the walls and a china dog smoked a joss-stick like a cigarette. Water was running upstairs. I cleared my throat and called Olga's name. The answering silence was eerie. I followed the echo to the top floor. The glow of the wall-radiator in the bathroom helped me locate the dripping tap. I turned it off and stood in the doorway of the main bedroom. The lights were out. All I could see was the vague shape of a bed and a glimmer where the mirror was. I groped for the switch and pressed down the button.

Olga Suchard was lying on her side with her eyes

closed. Her face was completely devoid of colour and the sheet covering the lower half of her body was soaked with blood. There was more blood on her nightdress, on her dangling outstretched arm, the towels in the basin on the floor. A bottle of antiseptic lay on the carpet overturned, the liquid soaking into a stain. I stepped over the basin and felt Olga's limp wrist. There was no pulse, no sign of breathing coming from her mouth. I lifted an eyelid and let it fall. There's a finality about death that's recognisable once you have seen it.

CHAPTER THREE

I picked up the phone on the bedside table and dialled. A man's voice responded immediately.

'Which service, please?'

'Police.'

'May I have your number, please?'

I gave it to him together with my name and the address. 'A woman's dead,' I explained to the following voice. 'I'll wait here till somebody comes.'

I put the receiver down. All I could find to drink was a bottle of Cyprus sherry. I poured some into a glass and went into the sitting room. Then I opened the shutters, dragged a chair to the window, sat down and waited. I kept away from the phone deliberately. I needed time to think before I talked to Anne. A few minutes went by and a squad-car howled down the street, blue light flashing. I reached the hallway at the same time as the doorbell rang.

The stocky man standing on the doorstep was wearing a greasy raincoat with the collar up about his ears. Rain glistened in his sparse sandy hair. He flashed the warrant-card concealed in his palm like a street-grafter displaying a hot watch.

'Detective Inspector Prior, Chelsea C.I.D.' The accent was Welsh. The way he announced his rank gave me the impression that it was newly come by. A couple of younger men stood behind him. All three pushed into the hallway, blocking my exit to the street. One of them shut the door and planted his back against it. Nobody spoke for a moment but Prior was shooting keen suspicious looks at me.

'My name is John Raven,' I said. 'I made the call.'

Prior acknowledged the introduction with one of his own. 'Detective Sergeant Leach.' His thumb indicated the man at his side. Leach nodded back familiarly. He was in his early thirties with a beer-drinker's face moulded into false good humour. His grey overcoat was too tight for him and he was wearing two-tone Hush Puppies.

'O.K.,' said Prior. 'Let's get on with it.'

I led the way upstairs. I reached the kitchen when I realised that the third man had stayed in the hallway. I addressed myself to Prior.

'Do you mind telling me what's going on, Inspector? I made the call, remember. There's no question of me making a run for it.'

He stood there blinking but he made no answer. I waited outside the bedroom till both Prior and Leach had gone in. The stench of blood and antiseptic was sickening. Prior opened the shutters and pulled down the window. He walked round the bed, looking at the dead girl and shaking his head. A strand of her hair lifted on the current of cool damp air. Leach shifted some things on the dressing table and leaned his buttocks on the top. I'd no idea how many deaths this pair had investigated but neither seemed particularly impressed.

Prior explored his nose with his thumbnail. 'Did you find the body?'

'I found the body.'

35

'Did you touch anything in here? Move anything?'
His lilting voice was knowing.

I took my time answering. 'I touched her wrist,' I
said finally. 'And her left eyelid. That was to determine
whether or not she was dead. You'll find my fingerprints on the phone and a bottle and glass downstairs.
The cheroot isn't mine.'

He took his thumb from his nose, wincing. He went
into the bathroom. I heard him opening and shutting
the drawers in the medicine-chest. Leach and I continued to outstare one another. Prior came back, very
Welsh and very sarcastic.

'Looks as though we've got a live one here, George,'
he said, wagging his head in mock admiration. 'An
amateur detective with all the answers.'

Mucus was worming from the dead girl's nostril and
I wished that someone would cover her face.

'I was eighteen years on the force,' I said quietly.
'Fourteen with C.I.D.'

Prior cocked his head. 'What did you say your name
was?'

'He said Raven,' Leach volunteered. 'John Raven.'

'How'd you get in here?' Prior asked keenly. 'Got your
own key, have you?'

I moved so that the dead girl's face was out of my
sight. 'I don't have my own key, no. This girl's name is
Olga Suchard and she worked for my sister. She was
supposed to be sick and her phone didn't answer so my
sister asked me to check. I was sitting outside in my
car when a man came out in a hurry, leaving the front
door open. That's how I got in.'

'Do you know how long this man was up here?'

I lit a cigarette. The smoke curled away from the

36

open window. 'I can't be sure. I was listening to the radio. But I'd say about twenty minutes, possibly a little more or less.'

Leach offered one of those let-me-be-your-friend grins. 'What did the guy look like?'

He continued to pick up pieces of silver from the dressing table, turning them upside down and searching for the hallmark as he talked.

'He was on the short side,' I answered. 'Fiftyish. Dark coat, no hat and carrying a leather bag. Almost certainly he was driving a Volkswagen. I'd know him again if I saw him.'

The two men exchanged quick glances. 'Spectacles. Was he wearing spectacles?'

'And trousers,' I said. I could see no reason to be over-respectful to this pair of clowns.

A car stopped on the street below. Prior stuck his head out of the window then turned to face us.

'It's Baxter,' he said to his partner. 'So we won't be hanging around. He'll want to get back to his dinner.'

I heard the street door being opened, the detective's respectful greeting, footsteps coming up the stairs. The police surgeon was a grizzled terrier of a man with a polkadot bow tie and a shaggy overcoat. He nodded at Prior and put his bag on the floor by the side of the bed. He bent over Olga's body, pulled the sheet back and gently parted the dead girl's knees. He made a face and pulled the sheet back.

'No mystery here,' he announced. 'Whoever performed was a man with some medical training—or possibly a woman. Someone who should have known what he was doing. The female anatomy is a delicate arrangement. You're working to narrow tolerances.'

37

He proceeded to the bathroom, ran water and washed his hands. He was holding a small phial in his hands when he came back.

'Any of you seen this before?'

We looked at one another questioningly. No one answered. The doctor gave the phial to Prior.

'Whoever it was left this behind. Pituitrin. It's an abortifacient. If it's used and something goes wrong, the pituitry glands won't show up in an autopsy. He'd have done a hell of a lot better with it than with an instrument. Poor girl. She can't be more than twenty, twenty-one.' He consulted his watch. 'Ah well, there's nothing more I can do. I'll notify the coroner's officer and send an ambulance. Goodnight to you.' His nod included the three of us.

Leach snorted as the police surgeon stomped downstairs. *'Abortifacient!'*

It did me good to put him right. 'Something that produces a miscarriage.'

Prior pulled the sheet up over the dead girl's face. 'I imagine you know the drill, Mr Raven. I'll have to ask you to come to the station and make a statement.'

Anything was better than staying in that room. 'The sooner the better,' I said. 'There is just one thing. Someone told me a string of lies about this girl tonight. Someone called Teresa Cintron. She also did her best to follow me home. You might like to ask her why. She's a student at the Cosmos School of Advanced English, that's Queen's Gate. I've got a hunch that she knows as much about this affair as anyone.'

'Get on it, George,' said Prior. Leach hurried down the stairs. Prior detailed the man in the hallway to wait for the ambulance and rode with me, climbing into the Citroën with exaggerated appreciation.

'French? This is real style. A car like this must cost a pretty penny.'

I gave him the exact sum. 'That's exclusive of Value Added Tax, of course.'

'Of course,' he agreed and leaned back, half-closing his ratty little eyes. 'John Raven. You know, that name does mean something to me. Left at the lights.'

'I know the way to Chelsea nick,' I said tightly.

He held up a warning finger. 'I've got it now. Detective Inspector Raven, wasn't it? Serious Crimes Squad under Commander Drake. Didn't you retire some time last year?'

It was obvious that he remembered more but comment was superfluous. Chelsea police station occupies a block just west of Sloane Avenue, in the heart of what is a fashionable residential neighbourhood. Their presence in the local pubs and shops isn't always appreciated. People tend to be nervous when surrounded by policemen. Prior directed me into an official parking-bay, grinning as if he'd just thought of something amusing. I followed him up the steps and under the blue lamp into another world. The fat desk sergeant looked up, leaning down hard on his elbows as he saw me. He shook his head.

'Goblimey, I always knew they'd get you in the end! How are you, mate?' He shoved out a hand.

It was an old acquaintance, onetime jailer at Marylebone Police Court and an expert on Cockney villainy.

'In good form,' I said. 'I thought they'd have put you out to grass by now.'

He closed a pale blue eye. 'Couldn't do without me,

39

mate.' He turned to Prior. 'Better watch this one, Inspector. He'll run bleedin' rings round you.'

Prior shook the rain from his coat. 'Don't worry about me, sergeant. You've got enough to do, taking care of yourself.'

My smile told the sergeant whose side I was on. 'I'll see you later, Bert,' I said and went up after Prior.

The C.I.D. room was on the second floor. I remembered it all too well. The smell of orange-peel and tobacco smoke, the porridge-coloured linoleum scarred with cigarette-burns, the Office of Works furniture, tables that served as desks and functional chairs. *Wanted* and *Reward* notices hung on the pea-green walls together with a dreary catalogue featuring engineering components.

Prior lowered the window-blinds and hung his wet coat in front of a miserable one-bar heater.

'Take a seat,' he invited, rubbing his hands together in the manner of an old-fashioned revivalist sizing up the house. He settled himself behind an ancient typewriter and fed paper between the rollers. He was giving the machine the first few tentative pecks when Sergeant Leach opened the door. Prior cocked an inquiring eyebrow.

'I found her,' said Leach. 'She lives in Tregunter Road. She's downstairs with the matron. It's Hannigan again.'

Prior's face showed pleasure. 'I *knew* I was right. Did you pick him up too?'

'Nope,' said Leach. 'But the girl downstairs made all the arrangements. She admits it.'

'Hannigan?' said Prior.

Leach shrugged. 'The woman he lives with says that

he left home at eleven o'clock this morning. She hasn't seen him since. I spoke to her on the phone. He was in that pub on the corner of Selwood Terrace at lunchtime and that's it. I've got the number of his car and I've put out a one-five-six.'

The name Hannigan meant nothing to me but a one-five-six was a code alarm signifying despatch and caution.

'The bastard can't get far.' Prior lit a filthy pipe and waved the stem in my direction. 'Let's have your full name, occupation and address.'

He punched the information on to the paper, using two fingers and two thumbs. 'John Havelock Raven, thirty-nine years old, of in-de-pen-dent means living on *Albatross*, Chelsea Reach. What's that, a hotel?'

'A houseboat,' I said. I must have made a thousand statements in my time but this was the first I'd made in similar circumstances.

I told them about Anne's telephone call and finished with mine to Scotland Yard. Prior gave me the typewritten statement to read through and sign. He put the two sheets of paper in a buff envelope and threw it in his OUT tray.

'There's one thing I don't understand,' he said in his singsong faraway voice. 'Why didn't you get in touch with us before, look? You knew the girl was supposed to report her change of address.'

I snapped my lighter shut. 'You're taking too much for granted. All I knew was that someone claiming to be from the Alien's Office telephoned my sister's house and asked to speak to Miss Suchard.'

'Yes, but...' Prior's voice died away as the door opened. A large belligerent-looking man with steel coloured hair surged in, using his eyes like darts. The 100-watt desk-lamp struck a shine from his blue serge suit.

'Commander Drake,' he announced. 'Who's in charge here?'

Prior whipped his pipe from his mouth. 'I am, sir. Inspector Prior.'

Drake stabbed a finger like a frankfurter at the sergeant. 'Name?'

Leach quivered to attention. 'Sergeant Leach, sir.'

'Shut that bloody door,' instructed the Commander. He whisked Prior's chair under his own broad butt and showed a couple of badly-discoloured teeth.

'Well now, John,' he said comfortably. 'This is a surprise.' He spoke in the manner of someone who hears of a friend's misfortune and comes to his side.

'Bollix,' I said. The time had long gone when I was required to show him either courtesy or respect.

Prior and Leach assumed looks of caution as if unsure whether or not they were hearing correctly. Drake took the outburst in his stride.

'Believe it or not, John, this is pure coincidence. I just happened to be in the Communications Centre checking some other business when I saw the call-in record. And there it was. A Mr John Raven notifying a death at ninety-eight Clare Street. I said to myself, I wonder if that could be *my* John Raven. And sure enough, it was!'

He smiled wistfully, picking up the buff envelope from Prior's out tray. He turned it over in his fingers then donned a pair of spectacles and began to read. He put my statement back in the envelope and shook his head.

'A bad business, John. You know, leaves a nasty taste in the mouth.'

From the way he said it I might have been the dead girl's lover or even the abortionist. Eighteen months had gone by since we'd last met in the Commissioner's office. Allies in name, Drake and I were enemies by instinct. There wasn't a single thing about me that he liked, including the way I did my job.

I looked across the desk at him. 'Still breaking people's backs, are you?'

He picked at his ear thoughtfully. 'You don't change do you, John?'

'Nor do you.' I turned to Prior. 'I'd like to go now.'

Prior glanced at Drake who lifted a shoulder. The gesture seemed to give Prior confidence.

'You're free to go whenever you want,' he said, waving at the door. 'There's only one thing more I need from you, your sister's address. What did you say her husband was, a lecturer at London University?'

'London School of Economics,' I corrected. 'But I'd like you to hold off on that till I've had a chance to speak to my sister. The news is going to come as a shock. She was fond of the girl.'

Drake was leaning back in his chair, eyes closed, whistling. Leach was by the door standing very straight, features composed in alert and watchful fashion. Drake suspended his whistling.

'Be reasonable, John. These officers are investigating a serious offence. And they're having to do it the hard way. We know what a brilliant detective you were but we don't all have your talents.'

I made sure that there could be no doubt about what

43

I was saying. 'I just made a decision. I'm not going to *give* you my sister's address.'

He made a noise like a thirsty buffalo arriving at a waterhole. 'That's being bloody stupid, John. Come on, now! It's easy enough to get the information.'

'Then get it,' I retorted. I'd taken a lot from him over five long years without knuckling under and I saw no reason to start now. I put my feelings into the sort of language that I knew would offend most. 'You've got as much right to be a Commander of the Metropolitan Police as a blue-arsed baboon. You're nothing but a Neanderthal man, a jealous conniving bastard.'

He opened his mouth very wide and gulped in air. 'Very good,' he said finally. 'Very good indeed! You see, Inspector, the advantages of a classical education. That's the sort of thing they're taught at Harrow.'

Prior was out of his depth and uncomfortable. 'Is there anything else on your mind, John?' asked Drake. 'Anything you'd like to add?'

'As a matter of fact there is,' I said. 'A rumour's going the rounds that I'm supposed to have been on the take. That I was allowed to resign rather than stink-up the fair name of the Serious Crimes Squad. Did you hear anything about that?'

He moved his head from side to side. 'I wish you hadn't brought that up, John. It's a subject that I'd sooner forget.'

'How *can* you forget?' I challenged. 'You started the rumour. If ever I'm in a position to prove it I'll sue you for the fucking bed you sleep on.'

I scraped my chair back and stood up. Leach barred my way to the door.

'You'd better know exactly what you're doing,' I warned.

He released his grip on the door handle in response to Prior's signal. Prior came outside on to the landing with me. A drunk was singing in the cells below.

'I'll let you know about the inquest,' the Inspector said cautiously. He was still unsure of me. 'You'll be wanted...'

I could see Drake through the open door, smiling like a clown at a carnival. The desk sergeant gave me an inquiring look.

'What's supposed to be going on up there, John?'

'I wish I knew,' I answered. 'I only wish that I knew.'

I sat in the car for a while, thinking about Drake. It was just possible that he was speaking the truth. Nosing around in the Communications Centre was in character, the sort of devious dodge that he'd think up. He was adept in making envy and suspicion look like nothing more than keen police work. In the old days he used to butter-up the clerks working in Criminal Records, finding out who was pulling whose file and why. He had more dirty tricks than a Turkish wrestler and the point was that if you worked under him you were supposed to be as dirty as he was. Either that or he broke you. It was as simple as that. I'm one of the few who has walked away comparatively unscathed and with a clear conscience.

I could work out why he had come to Chelsea. What I couldn't determine was what came next. I'd no idea how long I'd been in the police station. The pub was still open when I reached home. One of my reasons for buying *Albatross* was the barge's history. She'd been built no more than ten miles from where I was born and had nosed her way along the Grand Union Canal system, drawn by generations of powerful plodding horses. I like the thought of her, over a hundred years later, riding the river better than the pretentious modern craft around her.

I cooked myself bacon and eggs and put on a record. I was half-way through my food when the phone rang. It was Anne. Someone from Hampstead police station had just been round with the news. I don't think Anne's wept since her son cut his first tooth but she sounded desperately close to it now.

'How *could* she?' she wailed. 'Why didn't she confide in me? God knows I'd have done whatever I could to help. It's not as though I'm the sort of woman...'

I put the phone down on the table, my appetite gone. I could hear her voice buzzing in the diaphragm. I turned the record off and picked up the receiver again.

'... deceitful. I mean, who *is* this man? *Which one?* The man who made her pregnant of course. You can imagine what Jerzy is saying. You know how he hates anything to do with the police. Thank God the children were in bed when the officer came. What am I going to tell them, John?'

'You're going to tell them Olga's dead,' I said firmly. 'Sooner or later they're going to learn that people do die. Tell them she had an accident and keep them away from the newspapers.'

She sniffed. 'That's another thing. All the publicity.' She was probably sitting upstairs in her bedroom with the door locked. Jerzy would be in his study, reading philosophy. In moments of stress his mind took refuge in lofty sentiments. The sixteen feet of cord on my phone allows me to be mobile. I took the instrument into the kitchen and knocked the cap off a bottle of Budweiser. Anne needed someone to listen to her, someone to reassure her of her place in the best of all possible worlds.

'Look,' I said patiently. 'The girl's dead and there's nothing anyone can do about it. It's not your fault and it's not my fault. Let's start from there. The police will have notified the Swiss Embassy. You'll have to get in touch with her parents.'

'Her *parents*!' shrieked Anne. 'My *God*, I completely forgot. The policeman who came here said that I would have to attend the inquest.'

'We all will,' I said shortly. I'd be involved in this sordid affair because of her but I could hardly remind her of it. 'I've been with the police for the last couple of hours. I'm the one who found her body, remember.'

Her tone took on a touch of resilience. 'Can't you do something about keeping our names out of the newspapers, John?'

'Nothing,' I said flatly. Chilled beer-bubbles exploded against the backs of my teeth. 'And it won't stop at the coroner's inquest. There'll be criminal proceedings and we'll be involved. The police already know the name of the abortionist. It's a matter of time before they pick him up. He'll be tried for manslaughter.'

'Good God!' she said, feelingly. 'That poor poor girl. *John?*'

I emptied the last of the beer into my glass. 'I'm here.'

'You'll just have to do something,' she announced peremptorily. 'This man has to be found.'

'Didn't you hear what I said? The police know who

47

he is. Apparently he's an old hand at it. Some doctor who was struck off the Register.'

'I don't mean him,' she said impatiently. 'I'm talking about this other man. The one who got her pregnant.'

No one had mentioned him up to now except Anne. It was an odd thought. 'Yes, well it's been a long night and I'm bushed,' I said. 'I'll call you in the morning, O.K.?'

CHAPTER FOUR

I slept fitfully, waking to the sound of still more rain. I threw my poncho over my pyjamas and collected the newspapers from the box at the end of the gangway. The only piece of mail was a bill for records I had neither ordered nor received. I put it in the wastepaper basket, made coffee and spread the newspapers. There was no mention of Olga Suchard's death but I found an item in the stop-press column of the *Daily Telegraph*.

Ostend
Police here arrested Joseph Hannigan, 54, late last night. Hannigan described as a doctor and giving London address held on Scotland Yard warrant alleging manslaughter. Extradition proceedings likely to be formal. Escort on its way from London.

It was a quarter-past-eight and the Urbanovic household rose early. I took the phone off the hook and read the newspapers thoroughly. The weather forecast promised changeable weather. Some people in the Midlands were striking because the firm they worked for could no longer pay their wages. The pound had slid still lower. I looked through the windows. The gulls used the houseboats as launching-pads, scavenging like the pigeons that infested the streets. I called Anne at ten, cutting firmly through the account of what Jerzy had said to her and vice-versa to tell her that I was getting hold of George Ashley. George is our family lawyer and trustee. I wanted someone on our side to be present at the inquest. I caught him at the office and he promised to be available. I stayed on the houseboat all day, reading and listening to music. It was after five when the doorbell rang. I went out on deck. It was Drake. I could see the car that had brought him, a uniformed driver at the wheel. I looked Drake up and down.

'What the hell do you want?'

He shielded his face against the driving rain with his umbrella. 'Aren't you going to ask me in?'

He stood there, splaylegged and smiling, his big feet stuffed into rubber overshoes. He was wearing his usual serge with a Scotland Yard tie, a baggy overcoat with gamekeeper's pockets and the old black homburg. I thought of slamming the gangway door on his wartlike nose but I was curious. I led the way across the deck into the sitting room. He took off his hat and sat down, shifting the copy of *Pepys Diary* that I had been reading. His eyes took in the tea tray on the much-mended Aubusson carpet. A tug fussed upstream towing a string of coal barges. The wash left *Albatross* wallowing, the mooring chains creaking and groaning. My old sweater had holes, my jeans were dirty and I was glad that I hadn't shaved. It somehow pleased me to think that everything Drake saw he either loathed or didn't understand.

'About this inquest,' he said. 'It's tomorrow at ten-thirty a.m. Westminster Coroners' Court. You won't forget to be there?'

I lit a cigarette and leaned against the outside wall

where I could see his car. The driver had pulled in front of the pub.

'What *is* all this?' I demanded. 'I didn't know they sent people of your stature round with inquest summons. What's the matter, can't you find anything else to do?'

He leaned back and clasped his hands a couple of inches above his belly. The top three buttons on his flies were undone.

'I can find plenty to do but this is sort of special, isn't it.' He extracted an envelope and placed it on the table between us. 'Your formal invitation. Wear a tie and wash behind your ears.'

He was smiling the way he'd smiled the morning he'd knifed me in the Zaleski caper. It was supposed to have been the end of a feud that had started the day I'd joined his command. He'd been my Co-ordinator. He was one of the original Old Bills, a Mustachio Pete who had come up the hard way. A merciless cutter of corners dedicated to the pursuit of convictions at all cost, he hated my guts from the moment he laid eyes on me. Everything about me was an affront to him. My background, the fact that I lived on a houseboat in Chelsea, my appearance and my record at police college. Most of all he was afraid of me. I'll never know why.

'What is it?' I asked. 'What's on your mind? You can talk. There's nobody here but us.'

His jowls quivered as he shook his head. 'You and I have some unfinished business, John. A score to settle.'

I knew what he meant only too well. The Zaleski affair had made the headlines, a crime reporter's dream. All the ingredients were there. Three middle-aged Poles, ex-commandos, a jewelled monstrance with seven hundred and eighty-two gems in it, a master criminal the police had been after for years. Two governments were involved and the reputation of C Department was at stake. Drake had hung that monstrance round my neck like a halter and sat back and waited for me to commit suicide. Instead of which I'd wrapped up the case and captured a notorious villain. Drake's final humiliation had been to learn all this from the Commissioner himself.

I blew smoke at the floor. 'You're a dreamer, Drake. I'm a civilian in case you forgot.'

He wagged his head again, staring at the Paul Klee. 'Horrible,' he said. 'Yes, well Hannigan's going to be charged with manslaughter. You'll be chief witness against him. A good lawyer could make things awkward for you.'

'I think we're getting off the track here,' I suggested.

He grinned, enjoying himself. 'Someone who knew a bit of your background might attack your credibility. You know, things like your girlfriend committing suicide.'

I jerked the door open. Rain came in on the wind. 'Out!' I said curtly. 'Go before I beat your face in.'

He collected his hat and umbrella, standing close enough for his stale breath to register.

'I'll get you, John,' he promised. 'One of these days I'll get you.'

I knew that he'd try, nevertheless I felt better once he had gone. I reminded myself that there are Rules of Evidence, that an Old Bailey judge would come down heavily on any unjustified attempt to attack a witness's character. One thing remained crystal clear: Drake's hatred of me was as lively as ever. I put on Landowska playing harpsichord and gradually relaxed. About nine o'clock I opened a couple of bottles of Budweiser and sliced some salt beef. It was ten or more when I called Jerry Soo's home number. Jerry is Hong Kong-born and the only Chinese cop at the Yard—or at least he was in my day. We were at police college together and he was just as much a misfit as I was. This one incontrovertible fact started a friendship between us that somehow survived the years and my resignation. Jerry's the only link that I have with that particular past.

He lives on the top floor of a highrise block in Rotherhithe on the unfashionable side of the river, four miles downstream from *Albatross*. A Taiwan girl called Louise spends most weekends there. She's a cello player with the London Philharmonic Orchestra. Otherwise Jerry lives there alone with an Abyssinian cat and his stamp collection. He's been suffering my moods with philosophical cheerfulness for the last eighteen years. There may be men who are more reliable, readier with help when asked, but I've never met them.

'Jerry?' I asked and cocked my head on one side as the words whined and clicked from his nose.

'So solly, Mistuh Laven. Sheets still dutty.'

'Very good,' I said. 'Now listen to this. Guess who's walked back into my life like a big smelly bear.'

His voice changed to his normal impeccable English. 'I give up.'

'None other than our own Commander Drake. He walked into Chelsea nick last night as large as life, giving me the "John for it".'

'What the hell were you doing in the Chelsea nick?'

'That's a good question,' I admitted and told him why. 'Not only that, the bastard's just turned up here to deliver the summons to the inquest in person.'

I heard the click of dominoes and guessed that Louise was in the flat with him.

'Was anyone else there when you found the girl?' Jerry asked.

'Nobody. Look, Jerry, I'm a little bit worried about the Central Criminal Court. I don't want Cathy's name brought into it and Drake was doing some heavy hinting. You know, the suicide and that.'

His voice was charged with warning. 'Watch him, John. If he can screw you he will.'

'I already know that,' I answered. 'What's he doing these days? I mean what's his precise function?'

'He's a man of mystery,' he said solemnly. 'A feline figure moving through the underworld, his very shadow striking terror into the hearts of desperate criminals.'

I heard Louise's tinkle of laughter. 'You're brilliant,' I said. 'A wonderful comedian. Now tell me.'

'Are you sitting down?'

'I'm standing, why?'

'Then sit. A new squad has been created since your time to investigate charges of corruption in the Met. They're called "The Untainted" and they're into everything imaginable. They visit villains in the nick and take down long statements about naughty coppers. They find out how much money you have in the bank, bug your phone and read your mail. And the man in charge of the whole operation is none other than that stern but just officer, Commander Drake.'

'I don't believe it,' I said weakly.

'That's not all.' His voice seemed thin and far-away. 'The Commander doesn't mess with Assistant-Commissioners and Deputies. He's directly responsible to the Man himself.'

'That does it,' I exclaimed. 'Now I *am* going to sit. Thanks, Jerry. I'll be in touch.'

The following day was colder with the rain scudding on a north-east wind that reddened the noses of the people hurrying along the Embankment to work. I put on my blue velvet suit, a white shirt and the black tie I had worn to Cathy's funeral. I'd never worked on a murder or manslaughter case and it would be the first time that I put foot in a coroner's court. I hadn't been able to face it with Cathy. But I knew more or less how things worked. A coroner is obliged to convene a court if a person appears to have died a violent or un-natural death. And the coroner has to be a doctor, solicitor or barrister of no less than five years' standing.

It was ten o'clock by the time I arrived at Horseferry Road. A black Scotland Yard Jaguar was drawn up out-side the entrance to the red brick courthouse. It was the same car that Drake had used the previous evening. I could see the back of his head as he sat reading a news-paper. I drove past and parked around the corner. The long windowless building on the other side of the wall was the morgue. I locked the car and strolled back to the café on the corner. I wiped a spot on the steamed win-dow and sat watching the courthouse entrance, sipping a cup of what tasted like pure tannic acid. Previous infusions had eaten into the crockery and I had fears for my stomach-lining.

The first person I recognised getting out of a cab was the Venezuelan girl. Her outfit was too casual to have been bought for the occasion but the colour was right. Black shoes and stockings, a half-belted coat with a

55

swagger of white at the throat. I'd forgotten just how good her bone-structure was, the slightly hawkish nose and high, fine cheekbones. Her hair was covered with a scarf as if she was going to church. A squad car unloaded Prior and Leach, the Inspector wearing some kind of football scarf tucked into his overcoat. His junior had on a checked suit with his Hush Puppies and looked like a smalltime bookmaker trying to protect his credit.

Drake lowered his newspaper as the two detectives passed but neither he nor they made any sign of recognition. It was plain that Drake was going to attend the inquest but I'd no idea in what capacity. Probably no more than to sit there emanating evil as I gave my testimony. The rumour about me had started soon after I had left the force. Jerry Soo had been the first person to tell me about it. Someone else had mentioned it to him, knowing that he was a friend of mine. The story went that I had been caught redhanded taking a bribe from a fence called Godinsky. The account was fleshed-out with a wealth of personal detail that could only have come from someone with access to my personal file. It was perfectly true that I had been involved in a case with Godinsky. The jury found him Not Guilty. Two weeks later he was killed in a car crash, conveniently enough for whoever had started the rumour. Drake was the logical culprit. Whatever rules I had broken as a cop had been to do with discipline. I'd never as much as accepted a cigar from a thief and Drake knew it. The cases of scotch at Christmas, the tickets for fights and football-cup finals, the vouchers for junkets to the Caribbean, all had come my way at some time or other under the Old Pals Act with no specific favours asked. I'd always returned them to the senders, getting the slow shakes of the head and incredulous looks from less scrupulous colleagues. It was less a matter of expediency than of ethics and Drake must have known how the rumour would hit me. I meant what I'd said to him. If I could ever prove his slander I intended to file suit for the fillings in his teeth.

I pushed the cup of tea away and lit a cigarette. More people were going into the courthouse, a steady stream by now. Anne appeared in a cab with a middle-aged man in one of those boxy French-type suits who had to be the dead girl's father. George Ashley arrived in Savile Row pinstripes and a bowler hat, gliding from his Rolls on invisible rollerskates. I left a coin on the table and hurried across the street. The courtroom was up on the second floor. George Ashley was waiting for me on the landing, smelling of eau-de-Portugal and looking more like a stockbroker than a lawyer. There's a well-fed and self-assured manner about him that has little to do with the abstemiousness of the law. He put his dispatch-case on the ground and gave me a long firm handshake.

'How are you, John! Now don't worry. I've had a word with the Coroner and he's going to adjourn, of course. They always do in cases like this when criminal proceedings are pending.'

His smile was expansive and confident, an indication that with Ashley, Bates and Pettifer in your corner nothing in the world could ever go wrong. I dropped my cigarette end in the bucket of sand near the entrance and went into the courtroom. Drake was sitting just inside, arms folded and wearing an I-am-here-to-see-justice-done look.

I turned, noticing that George Ashley was still outside. 'Where are you going, George?' I asked. 'You're not thinking of leaving, are you?'

A frown tugged at his forehead as if he were suddenly in pain. 'I don't get all this, John. What seems to be the trouble? I spoke to the coroner's officer last night. These chaps are always well-informed. Everything seems to be perfectly straightforward as far as you and Anne are concerned. No problems at all.'

'It's possible,' I said. 'In which case I shall have paid you for nothing. But you stay.'

A pleasant-faced usher showed me to a high-backed bench across the aisle from Drake. Prior and Leach were sitting a few yards away, Anne and Olga's father with the Cintron girl on the far side of the room. There were a dozen or so student nurses in court, blacks and Asians, all of them alert and with notebooks. At close quarters Teresa Cintron looked as if she hadn't slept for a week. The small half-panelled courtroom was warm and had bright overhead lighting. The usher closed the entrance-door and sat down next to the stenographer. Another door opened and the Coroner ambled in. He was a tall bony man with a stoop, dressed in tweeds and wearing a rosebud in his lapel. He directed a little bow at the jury and spoke in a clear light voice with beautiful diction.

'I understand, ladies and gentlemen, that you decided by wish of a majority not to view the body of the deceased?'

The foreman was one of those individuals determined not to be overawed by authority.

'That is correct,' he said briskly.

The Coroner inclined his head. 'Well, it is my duty to

tell you yours, ladies and gentlemen. I shall examine the witnesses under oath but it will be your verdict that sets forth who the deceased was and how and where she met her death and if by manslaughter the person or persons you find to be guilty. If that's quite clear, the usher will administer the oath to you.'

The usher was more like a golf club secretary welcoming the five men and two women as new members. The smallness of the room, the absence of wigs and gowns, gave the proceedings an air of informality. There was none of the tension of a criminal court. It was as if everyone present had decided to treat death as a friend rather than as an enemy. A monocle swung by a cord round the Coroner's neck. He fixed it in his left eye and consulted the papers in front of him.

'Mr Suchard?'

The man next to Anne stood up. 'I am.'

The Coroner smiled gently. 'I understand that you speak some English, Mr Suchard. Are you quite sure that you do not require the services of an interpreter?'

Suchard shook his head. 'I have enough English, thank you.' He made his way to the stand, wearing a black ribbon across the lapel of his jacket and looking determined. Paul Suchard stated that he was a research chemist working in Montreux. He had seen the body of the deceased which was that of his only daughter, Olga Marie, born in Grenoble on 21 January, 1955. She had come to England the previous year to study the language. She was not engaged to be married and as far as he knew she had no steady male companion. He gave his evidence clearly and with dignity, speaking with a strong French accent.

Anne came next, answering the questions promptly

and without emotion. The dead girl had worked for her as a children's help and up to the previous May she had lived as one of the family. She was well-mannered, completely honest and truthful. Apart from attending language classes in the evening she rarely went out, spending the time in her bedroom, painting and reading. My sister's voice hardened. In May Olga had decided to share a flat with a friend. Anne wasn't aware of any romantic entanglement. Had she suspected any she would have made it her business to find out who and what the man was. She felt that she had a responsibility to Olga's parents.

The monocle dropped from the Coroner's eye. 'Thank you, Mrs Urbanovic.'

Anne left the witness box surrounded by an aura of moral rectitude. It seemed indelicate for me to remember her teenage antics. She claimed her handbag from the bench where she had been sitting and signalled Suchard to leave. The usher got to the door first. I could see him explaining that witnesses had to stay in court until they were officially released. Her face took on an expression of extreme irritation and I knew what she would be thinking. She had done her duty and now she wanted to go.

The pathologist's evidence was short and technical. He had examined the body of a woman in her early twenties. The body was well-nourished though ensanguinated. Heart, lungs, liver and kidneys showed no sign of disease or exterior damage. The uterus was enlarged and flaccid. Large venous sinuses were open. An instrument had been used to rupture and axtravasate the uterine contents. Death would have occurred within fifteen to thirty minutes and was due to massive haemorrhage. The pathologist closed his notebook, blew his nose and looked at his watch.

'With respect, sir, I have a consultation at half-past-eleven.'

The Coroner did some mental arithmetic. 'Yes, of course, Doctor,' he said hurriedly. 'I'll bind you over. The usual conditions.'

I met Anne's look and shrugged. She would never admit that a doctor's time might be of more importance than her own. My name was called and I made an affirmation instead of taking the oath. Drake always hated me doing it. Defence lawyers sometimes imply that a readiness to lie is attached to my godlessness. However, I lost my faith the night Cathy swallowed a bottle of barbiturates. The Coroner read from his notes in his high clear voice.

'You are Mr John Raven residing on the *Albatross* houseboat moored in Chelsea Reach. You are thirty-nine years of age and of independent means?'

His questions were rhetorical, an invitation for me to reassert what I had already said in my statement. Drake listened with his arms folded, looking down at his pudgy fingers and smiling faintly. There was nothing offensive in his manner unless you happened to know the man. Prior and Leach were frankly bored, shifting their feet and yawning. I could see George Ashley taking notes with an old-fashioned fountainpen. I was conscious that told in open court parts of my story sounded curious. Some of the student nurses had their heads together and I sensed their curiosity. The Coroner dismissed me courteously, without comment. Leach winked as I pushed by to take my seat, wiping my sticky palms on my handkerchief. Teresa Cintron was next on the stand, tying her knots, her voice on the edge of defiance. Olga Suchard had been her friend and had confided that she was pregnant. Teresa had heard of a doctor who had been struck off the Medical Register and who performed abortions for a hundred and fifty pounds. She'd lent the dead girl part of the money and supplied Hannigan's telephone number. She'd no idea personally when or where the abortion was supposed to take place. The last time she had seen Olga was the morning preceding her death. There was no mention of the fact that she had spoken to me, nothing about trying to follow me home. I wasn't exactly surprised. In spite of her evasions she was the one who had procured Hannigan. She could – maybe should – have been charged as an accessory. But she was the Crown's principal witness and she'd obviously been promised immunity.

The Coroner closed his file and addressed the jury once Prior and Leach had said their pieces.

'There will be no need for your verdict today, ladies and gentlemen. I am adjourning this inquest until the results of proceedings in a criminal court are known. All interested persons will be properly notified. Thank you.'

He smiled, looking like a benevolent heron, and left the courtroom. I was the first to follow, waving quick farewell to Anne and Ashley and taking the steps down two at a time. I don't know why but I wanted to get the hell out of there. I was suddenly aware that someone behind was calling my name. A woman's voice echoed in the well of the stairway.

'Please, Mr Raven! Please wait!'

I slowed a little but kept on walking. I'd no idea what Teresa Cintron could want with me but with Drake on our heels it could wait until we got outside.

I stopped on the corner. The short street was a sort of kitchen for the surrounding office blocks with sandwich bars and cafés. Teresa came flying after me, jostling her way through the crowd. She had taken off her scarf in spite of the intermittent rain and tied it to her handbag. Exertion left her short of breath. She steadied herself in the doorway, fingering the gold crucifix on her breast. Her face was wet, her long hair lank but she remained a very attractive woman.

'Please,' she gasped. 'I must speak to you.'

I could see Drake's head fifty yards away. He was standing by the side of his car, chatting to Prior and Leach. I pulled her out of his line of vision.

'Speak to me about what?'

'Please,' she repeated. 'There is no one else I can talk to.'

I opened the door of the café. Tables had been laid for lunch but it was still too early for the noon rush. We found seats at the back of the room. There was no law against witnesses consorting that I'd ever heard of but with Drake all things were possible.

'Would you like something to drink?' I asked. 'Tea or coffee?'

She moved eloquent shoulders. Her eyes had the brilliance of old jade.

'A coke, please, if they have it.'

I bought a couple of bottles at the counter and carried them back to the table. I offered her a cigarette and she accepted, blowing smoke nervously as I pointed a finger at her.

'Let's start with you following me the other day. What was all that about?'

Her lighter was gold with her initials engraved on the

casing. She flicked it open and shut, avoiding my eyes.

'Olga was my friend and I knew that that man was going to her flat. Suddenly there you were at the school asking questions about her. I was frightened.'

'You told them in court that you didn't know when the abortion was taking place.'

She locked her eyes on to mine but stayed silent. I loosened my tie. It was the first time in weeks that I had worn one and the café was overheated.

'You didn't tell the Coroner that you followed me either, did you?' I challenged.

She shook her head. 'That was because the detective told me not to—Inspector Prior. He said it was unimportant.'

'What else did he tell you?' The answer could be interesting.

A couple of teenage louts lounged to the neighbouring table. One of them put his feet up on a chair and let go with a wolf-whistle, leering at Teresa. I kicked the chair away deliberately.

'Out!' I snarled. 'Your mother's looking for you!'

They looked at one another then vanished. 'What else did Prior tell you not to say?' I demanded.

Her eyes were steady now. 'Nothing. He kept asking me whether or not you knew Olga well. I said I didn't know. I told him that I'd never seen you in the flat.'

I gave her the benefit of the doubt. 'I suppose you realise that you're partly to blame for your friend's death?'

She took a deep breath. 'Of course I realise it! The police keep telling me that there will be no trouble for me but for the rest of my life I know I will suffer *here*.' She touched the cross on her breast.

She was the sort of girl who probably would. I knew the feeling. To care for someone and assume responsibility for her death is a cancer that time can control but never cure.

I used her first name without thinking. 'Tell me about it, Teresa. Tell me what's bothering you.'

She stabbed the cigarette at the ashtray. 'She was my only friend and now I am alone. I am twenty-five years old and in love with a man whose children I cannot bear. Do you know what that means to a woman, Mr Raven?'

The question implied a lack of sensitivity on my part and as such irritated me.

'What's that got to do with Olga's death?' I asked.

'I am very much alone,' she said quietly. 'Sergio is five thousand miles away and for me there is no one to talk to any more. No one I can trust.'

Her voice and manner rang true but I have never been the best judge of a woman's character. I was wary.

'Why pick on me? We don't even know one another.'

She raised dark green eyes. 'I trust you now. Surely that is a beginning.'

I drank the last of the coke. The address she had given in court was a fashionable one, a street near the Boltons. Her clothes were expensive and there was the gold lighter and late-model sports car. Everything pointed to a moneyed background. The way she looked at me dulled my critical faculty. Whatever the reason, it was flattering to have her interested in me.

'I'll help you if I can,' I said quietly.

Her hand found mine across the table, relief flooding into her face. The pressure of her fingers was warm and firm.

'Thank you. I just have to talk to someone. These detectives, Inspector Prior and the other one—whatever they do for me is because they have to. I realise it is necessary for their case. I am not entirely a fool.'

'You're a key witness.' I weighed air in my palms and let one hand plummet. 'You're the weight around Hannigan's neck.'

She moved her head from side to side. 'It's not that. It's the bag I want to talk about.'

I tried to blow a smoke-ring and failed. 'The bag.'

'The one Olga's boyfriend left at Clare Street. You see, he went to Zürich three days ago and he gave her this bag to take care of. He didn't even know that Olga was pregnant. She never told him. I can understand why – some men dislike the thought of having children. Olga was scared of losing him. She had it all worked out that she would be free of the baby by the time he came back from Switzerland. He would never have known.'

There was something about her story that didn't sound quite right. 'Why leave a bag with Olga? Why not leave it in his own home or take it with him?'

She lifted her hands and shoulders. 'She didn't tell me. She was so secretive about anything to do with him. All I knew was that his first name was Paul. I never even saw a picture of him. She was always worrying about compromising him. That's why she didn't want anything of his to be in the flat when Hannigan came. Just in case. The flat below hers is empty and she had the keys. Someone was supposed to be coming to fix floorboards and the agents had left the keys with her. Olga hid Paul's bag down there and gave the keys to me. If anything went wrong ... if she had to go to hospital ...' Her voice broke.

'Blow your nose,' I said and gave her my handkerchief.

She pulled herself together, producing a smile that was almost convincing.

'I'm sorry. It won't happen again. Anyway if Olga did have to go to hospital for some reason or other I was to get the bag and put it back in her flat. It had to be here when Paul returned from Zürich. That was important. He had his own keys.'

I shook my head, mystified. 'And you mean that you haven't told the police any of this?'

Her expression hardened. 'I don't *like* these men. The young one especially. He keeps making excuses to come to my flat.'

The news didn't surprise me at all. She was an alien and vulnerable. Someone like Leach might be expected to make the most of it.

'What sort of man is this Paul? She must have told you something about him. Where he lives for instance.'

She clicked her tongue, signifying no. 'Olga was strange in some ways. She felt that people smothered her. First her parents then your sister. And all the time Olga was dreaming of her Prince Charming, the man who would some day take her by the hand. Once she found him she wasn't going to let him go. She protected him against the world. In the end she gave her life for him.'

It was a romantic statement yet true. The idea touched off a secret resentment for the men and women who skate through life completely untouched by a sense of responsibility. It isn't so much that they avoid it. The very nature of their genes and chromosomes cauterises all consideration for others. Protected by their selfishness these people seem to attract the defenceless. Olga's boyfriend sounded like a first class example of the breed.

Teresa was still hanging on to my handkerchief which was smeared with her green eyeshadow.

'I'm sorry,' she said, looking down at it. 'I'll wash it for you.' It seemed ungracious to tell her that I had two dozen of them bought and embroidered by the Ursuline Sisters, a tribute to the recovery of an alleged Murillo stolen from their chapel. If nothing else, the incident taught the good sisters to be less trusting in devout strangers with a wish to pray long and alone.

She put the handkerchief in her handbag and produced a couple of door keys on a ring.

'I'll take those,' I said and opened her unresisting fingers. 'There's nothing more you can do for Olga. The time's come to start looking after yourself. I'm going to collect that bag and put it back upstairs for you. Don't worry about the keys. I'll see that they're returned to the agents. Would you like a piece of advice?'

She nodded, wide-eyed. 'Take your mind off Sergio,' I said. 'A love that makes you miserable isn't worth having.'

I didn't know how she was going to take it but a smile invested her eyes with sudden brilliance. She grabbed my hand again and pressed it against her cheek before I could stop her.

'Thank you for what you have done. You are a kind man.'

The Italian behind the tea-urn was watching us closely but she hung on to my fingers. It was the gesture of someone in need and, coming from her, difficult to ignore. I freed myself gently from her grip. Behind the

68

show of sophistication she was as vulnerable as her dead friend. I tore a sheet from my diary and scribbled my address and telephone number on it. I folded the slip of paper and put it in her bag.

'Hang on to this. You'll find me there most of the time. Whenever you feel like a chat or a drink. Or both.'

She nodded and left. I was glad that she went when she did. The next move would come from her and if it didn't, well it would probably stop me from making a fool of myself yet again.

CHAPTER FIVE

I gave her a few minutes before walking to the car. My sister was waiting there with Suchard. She hurried forward.

'Where on earth have you been? We've been standing here for hours. John, you'll have to talk to him. He's terribly upset. He's got it into his head that this business in the Coroner's Court is the end of everything. I've been trying to tell him that Hannigan will be punished but he doesn't seem to understand.'

I spoke to Suchard in French. 'Where are you staying?'

'The Plantagenet Hotel, Piccadilly. This is an outrage, Monsieur. My daughter has been murdered and nothing is done. I shall not let it rest.' He was stiff-faced with anger.

I touched Anne's arm. 'You'd better go home. I'll drive Mr Suchard to his hotel.'

She gave him her hand. 'I'm so sorry. I really am. I only wish there was something we could do. Please call if you need me. You have my telephone number.'

Suchard and I sat in the car. It took me twenty minutes to explain the niceties of British justice, the foregone conclusion that Hannigan would be convicted and sent to jail for a long term. He listened intently and I could feel his taut body relaxing inch by inch. He lit his cigarette with an ancient zippo and looked me full in the face.

'She was all I had, Monsieur. This man corrupted her.'

I thought he was talking of Hannigan then I realized he meant the dead girl's lover.

'He'll pay,' I assured him. 'You don't go through life trampling on other people's feelings without paying for it one way or another.'

I didn't believe it for a second but what else do you say to a man whose only daughter is dead, toppled from her virginal pedestal. The lines about his mouth hardened.

'I hope so, Monsieur. I believe myself to be a Christian but for this man I feel no charity.' He brooded for a moment before going on. 'They have given me the keys to Olga's apartment. What should I do, Monsieur? I cannot face those rooms and I must return to Switzerland.'

'Have the keys sent to my sister. She'll take care of everything.'

I dropped him off at his hotel and drove straight to Clare Street. It was getting on for one o'clock and a couple of bottles of milk stood next to the hydrangea on Olga Suchard's doorstep. I looked up at her bedroom. The white shutters were open. I wondered if the mess up there had been cleaned. Death is rarely tidy. Someone always has to take care of what is left behind, stop the milk deliveries, have the light and the phone disconnected. I could understand Suchard not wanting to face whatever was in his daughter's apartment. Anne's approach would be less emotional.

A yellow telephone-repair truck drew up on the other side of the street. The negro at the wheel had a head of hair like a black dandelion gone to seed. He watched idly as I let myself in through the front door of ninety-

71

eight. A letter was lying on the mat in the hallway. It was addressed to Mlle Olga Suchard and postmarked Zürich. The door at the top of the blue-carpeted stairs was shut. They had used a stretcher to bring the dead girl's body down. The handles had gouged the wall in places.

I used the second key that Teresa had given me to unlock the bottom flat. On the left was a sitting room with curtained windows overlooking the street. The kitchen on the right was bare except for a gas-stove. A partly-raised venetian blind offered a glimpse of the mews behind the house. The carpets had been removed but underfelt was still tacked to the boards. I went down to the basement. The bag was on the lavatory-seat in the bathroom. The windows were frosted and it was difficult to see. I carried the bag up to a better light. It was an elegant Edwardian affair, varnished black with tan leather trimmings. A faded label advertised some forgotten Baltic steamship line. I lowered my head suddenly, sniffing at the marzipan odour that was coming from the bag.

Back in the sixties, an enthusiastic Commissioner of Police had inaugurated a scheme officially named 'Adjuncts to the Analysis of Crime'. It consisted of lectures given during the summer vacation in universities and polytechnics up and down the country. The instructors were top men in their given fields and the courses were open to detectives of the rank of sergeant and over. I chose Explosives for the simple reason that Sussex University was only twenty-odd miles away from Glyndebourne. I could finish my class, change and be there on each night of the opera festival. There was an examination at the end of the course and I must have passed though much of what I learned was soon for-

familiar odour of burned paraffin. I cut myself a salt beef sandwich and drank a glass of milk. There'd been little to pack when I'd cleared my room at the Yard but one of the things I'd taken with me had been Bottles Bertorelli's presentation-pack. I unlocked the bureau-drawer in my bedroom and extracted the velvet-lined jewel-case. It contained some of the best skeleton keys ever made in England, lockpicks fashioned from surgical steel, forceps and a variety of master-keys for Yale-type locks and mortises. The way they had come into my possession was curious. Bottles was yet another of those thieves destined to take their last falls with me. I'd sent him to the Island for seven but he bore me no malice. As it turned out he served less than two and died in Parkhurst Prison Hospital. A few weeks later a parcel arrived at the Yard addressed to me. There was no letter enclosed, just the box with the burglar's tools. I made some inquiries at the jail and found that Bottles' sister had visited him at the last. The law-abiding have no monopoly when it comes to a sense of humour. I chose a selection of the smaller keys and remembered the envelope in my pocket. I opened it. The letter was written on the notepaper of the Baur-au-Lac Hotel and dated three days previously.

My darling:
I have been thinking of you so much and counting the moments till we are together again. My business here is almost finished and I will be back in London on Friday *for sure*. I'll call you from Heathrow as soon as I arrive. Now listen *carefully*, I want you to pack a bag with the minimum of clothes in it and be ready to leave England early on Saturday. Don't say a word

of this to ANYONE and that includes Teresa. This is
the beginning of everything for us, my darling. Every
hope we ever had for the future is about to come true.

I love you, my sweetheart. Remember that and
TRUST me!

Paul

It was a touching letter if you excluded the fact that
the writer had planted a bag of explosive on an innocent
girl. I locked the letter away in the bureau and changed
into jeans and sweater. I wasn't quite sure how I should
play this one. I was thinking about Drake, of course,
and how to defeat him. The fact that Olga's seducer
was a lawbreaker gave an edge to my moral indignation.
I don't suppose my feelings went much deeper at that
stage. I was pretty sure that the bag did contain gelignite and resolved to find out. There might be some clue
inside the bag that would help to identify its owner.
There was a certain satisfaction in the thought that
here I was, no longer on the force, yet still doing their
bloody work for them.

The house on Clare Street looked exactly as I had left
it. I let myself in again. I tried four keys before I found
the right one. The gelignite was packed in heavy-gauge
plastic bags, sixteen pounds of it. There was a box of
detonating-caps, the type with tetryl booster-charges, a
roll of electrical cable and a six-volt battery. I felt in the
pockets in the lining but they were empty. There was
a phone on the bare floorboards. I picked it up instinctively. My first intention was to call Jerry Soo for
help. My mind was picking its way like a cat through a
puddled farmyard. I was conscious only of two things,
the excitement of the chase and Drake's leering face.

The phone was dead. I put it down as someone opened the front door. I relocked the bag and ran it downstairs, replacing it in the lavatory. I stood by the back door, ready to go. Footsteps crossed the hallway and continued on up to Olga's flat. The house seemed very quiet. A series of bangs and thuds started overhead as if someone was searching the rooms. It continued for some time then the footsteps came down again. The visitor reached the hallway at the same time as I did. No more than a half-inch thickness of painted wood separated us. I heard the front door open and shut and reached the letterbox flap just in time to see the back of the man who had left. His long straight fair hair flapped as he bounced away on the balls of his feet. He was wearing a suede jacket over brown check trousers. He crossed the street to a dark-blue Ford Capri and opened the door on the driver's side. There was someone else sitting in the passenger seat but I couldn't see who. The blond-haired man was talking animatedly with his companion as the car drove off. I took a chance on being seen and sprinted for the Citroën. I caught up with my quarry at South Kensington. Traffic lights held us in front of the Underground station. A number thirty bus separated the two cars. The Capri turned left, back the way we had come, in the direction of Old Brompton Road. I was virtually sure that the driver was Olga's boyfriend and I had a good idea where he was going. The phone call earlier must have come from him. He'd arrived at Heathrow to get no answer from Olga, to find the flat empty and the bag he'd left with her missing. I could imagine how he was feeling. It was probable that he knew where Teresa lived and this was where they were heading.

She'd given her address in court and I knew it well. Tregunter Road runs at an angle from the church that bisects the Boltons. It's a quiet neighbourhood and most of the large Victorian houses have been converted into expensive flats. The Capri stopped a hundred yards ahead of me. I pulled in on the east side of the church and slid down in the driver's seat. The blond-haired man opened a gate and climbed the steps. It was a house fronted by beech trees that in summer would screen it from the street. Now they stood, dripping scarecrows against the leaden sky. The blond-haired man spoke into the voicebox. Seconds later the front door opened and he disappeared inside. His passenger eased himself out of the Capri. He was a slight man dressed in drab inconspicuous clothing. He strolled a few yards looking up at the windows of Teresa's house. Suddenly he wheeled sharply so that anyone behind him must have been seen. I recognised the hare's mouth set in a supercilious sneer immediately. There had been a time when this face had been printed on the minds of every C.I.D. man in the Metropolitan area. The Ratcatcher, alias George Burns, was a Glasgow-born safebreaker and gelignite expert, as cunning and vicious as the rodent that gave him his nickname.

The sobriquet stemmed from a stretch in Peterhead Jail during which Burns caught and tamed rats, carrying them about in his pockets much as a child does with a hamster. Seven years had gone by since he'd brought a team south to blow the vaults of the Westminster Safety Deposit. Some radio ham had picked up their conversation as they talked to one another on walkie-talkies. The eavesdropper had communicated with the police and the Ratcatcher had gone inside for ten years.

That he was walking the street meant that he'd out-smarted the parole board.

I kept my head low till he had climbed back into the Capri. It was five minutes or so before his companion appeared, hurrying from the house and restarting the motor. Once again, there was no doubt in my mind where they were going. No doubt either that it was simply a matter of time before the Ratcatcher realised that someone was on his tail. I headed back to Clare Street taking the shortest way. The telephone repair truck was still parked opposite number ninety-eight. I tucked the Citroën in behind it and slid down low on my shoulderblades. Moments later the Capri turned the corner. The blond man crossed the street shielding himself from the rain with a newspaper. He used his key and closed the door behind him. I was close enough to hear the wood splinter as he shouldered his way into the bottom flat. He was out again almost immediately, carrying the black-varnished bag.

What came next happened so smoothly it might have been rehearsed. A cab pulled up twenty yards away, discharging a woman with an armful of shopping. As the cab started off again, the Ratcatcher jumped from the Capri, flagged down the driver and was gone. Worse still, he was gone with the bag. The manoeuvre was so smoothly carried out that it caught me flatfooted. I didn't know whether to stay with Paul or follow the cab. Burns was wily and experienced. With his record possession of just one detonating-cap was enough to put him back in the slammer for years. Yet I knew him to be carrying enough explosive to blow up Nelson's Column. This suggested two things to me. That Burns was on the verge of pulling a caper and that this particular batch of gelignite was essential to the job. This was why he was taking the risks.

I followed the cab, trying to forget the precautions that had been taken at the time of the Ratcatcher's arrest. The area had been sealed off and the D11 boys brought in. D11 is a force of heavily-armed police marksmen. Burns was more than just a safebreaker. He was a cunning, determined villain with the reputation of stopping at nothing in order to preserve his liberty. He'd come out of the vaults carrying spare sticks of explosive and threatening to blow up the entire neighbourhood. It took a cop on a roof to put a bullet through his thigh.

I caught the cab at the next set of lights. They changed to green. I kept the Citroën hidden as best I could getting the occasional glimpse of Burns through the rear window of the cab. He was being driven east towards Knightsbridge. It was stretching credibility to reason that Olga's boyfriend hadn't known exactly what was in the bag he had left with her. The mere appearance of the bag made it likelier that it was his rather than the Ratcatcher's. The concept of guilt by association has always made sense to me. It's natural for a mother to say that her boy has been led astray but, like gold, bad company is where you find it. Since Olga's boyfriend hadn't known about the impending abortion he'd have felt quite safe about leaving the gelignite at Clare Street while he went to Zürich. Why he had gone and what he meant by 'the beginning of a dream come true' was something else again. Paul must have induced Teresa to talk. Reason and instinct told me that she wasn't part of the action. Somehow he'd forced the truth from her. By now he knew that Olga was dead

79

and probably that I had the keys to Clare Street.

Red lights halted us at Beauchamp Place, holding the six lanes of traffic as pedestrians scampered across the road. Suddenly I saw the Ratcatcher get out of the cab, the bag clasped in his right hand and thrusting money at the driver with his left. Then he was gone, vanished into a forest of umbrellas in front of Harrods. It happened so quickly that there was nothing I could do about it. The lights changed to green and the motorists behind me started leaning on their horns. I slammed across to the kerb, jumped from the car and sidestepped back through swerving traffic into the warm scented air of the department store. Mirrors reflected the display of men's clothing. The counters and aisles were crowded. I scanned anonymous faces but there was no sign of the man I was chasing. There were ten different exits that he might well have used. I made my way back to the car. I must have left the motor running in my haste and the wipers were still working. I drove up Kensington Gore to the battery of phone booths behind the Albert Hall. I called Jerry Soo's office at the Yard and spoke to his sergeant. It was the Inspector's weekend off and he'd already left for home. I tried the Rotherhithe number and got an answering service. Mr Soo would be absent until nineteen hours. Any messages for him would be recorded. I replaced the receiver, ignoring the tapping on the glass from outside.

I thought of calling Criminal Records and asking them to pull the Ratcatcher's file for an address, the names of known associates. I was familiar with the jargon customarily employed. The trouble was that too many ex-cops turned inquiry-agents had been doing the same kind of thing. A Sunday newspaper had recently run a feature article attacking this unwarranted use of confidential information. C.R.O. had instituted a new system of dealing with telephone-checks. They took the name and rank of the caller and telephoned back on an official number.

The tapping on the glass increased in intensity. The woman responsible was wearing what looked like the pelt of an Old English Sheepdog. I turned my back on her mouthing. The feeling of frustration grew as I thumbed through the directory, looking for Teresa Cintron's phone number. The most sensible thing for me to do was to get back in the car and drive away from the whole bloody mess. I wasn't a cop any longer but a private citizen. But come to that a private citizen had obligations as well as rights. I knew that a felony was being planned and it was my duty to inform the police about it. And the police meant Drake. According to Jerry Soo, as the head of A10 Drake could stick his nose anywhere. News about the Ratcatcher would be channelled through to the Yard immediately. I couldn't bear the thought of Drake extracting any sort of benefit from an action of mine. What I had to do was get hold of Jerry Soo as soon as possible and work out an alternative.

I tried Directory Inquiries. The operator was regretful. 'Teresa Cintron? I'm sorry, caller, but we have nobody of that name listed at this address.'

I hung up and opened the door. The woman outside blocked my way. 'You've been in there for almost twenty minutes,' she snapped. 'Why don't you try to have a little more respect for others!'

She was the sort of woman who follows you through revolving doors and comes out ahead.

'Madam,' I said at my politest. 'I do try but people like you make it difficult.'

I drove back to Tregunter Road and parked outside Teresa's house. Her name was on a plate above the bell-push. I pressed the button. A small voice tinkled below in the basement area. I peered down through the railings.

An eight-year-old girl stared up at me reprovingly, her freckled nose wet under a yellow sou'wester hat.

'It's no good ringing *her* bell. She's gone out.'

Having a niece of that age has taught me the value of the indirect approach. I assumed what I hoped was the right sort of smile.

'Hi! What's your name? Mine's John.'

She gave it some thought before answering. 'Kirstie Melinda MacDonald. Can you whistle like this?' She let go with a piercing blast produced through a gap in her front teeth.

I shook my head, my ears ringing. 'I bet you know the man who came to fetch Teresa.'

She shrugged indifferently and put her heel firmly on some sort of insect.

'My sister's prettier than Teresa anyway. And Teresa's a Venezoolan.'

'It was a man in a blue car wasn't it?' I suggested cunningly. A fair strand was hanging underneath her hat. 'Hair the same colour as yours.'

'I can wash my own hair,' she answered smugly.

I was getting grimmer by the second. 'You saw him, didn't you?'

A woman called from inside the house. The small girl opened the basement door.

'I have to go now,' she said in a prim voice. 'Goodbye.'

CHAPTER SIX

I sat in the car, trying to get my thoughts straight. I had a hunch that there wasn't going to be much time and it would be seven o'clock before I could contact Jerry. I'd remembered the Capri registration numbers but this wouldn't help. The licensing body wouldn't give the details of ownership unless I could produce some authority to back my request. Suddenly I remembered the Bishop. If anyone could help me he could. It was too early for him to be in his usual haunts and I had no idea where he lived. I drove to St James's and parked. I spent the next hour or so looking at books until the shops closed. It was just after six o'clock when I walked into the warm, discreetly-lit lobby of the St James's and Albany Hotel. It's a small establishment tucked away between St James's and Piccadilly and facing Green Park. The service and food are said to be excellent. Most of the guests are Americans with literary connections, some of the more restrained members of the acting profession and what newspapers describe as 'television personalities'. It's an atmosphere in which the Bishop flourishes. I've never determined what arrangements an ex-conman can make with a respectable house-detective but the Bishop seems to treat the hotel as his home. He doesn't exactly sleep on the premises but he picks up his mail there and signs for his drinks at the bar.

I eased through a group of expensively-gowned American women smelling of Estée Lauder. The clerk at the desk looked up, eyeing my jeans and sweater sharply. I smiled to give him confidence, hoping that he'd take me for a film director. The Bishop was in his usual seat in the Gambrinus Bar, as benign looking as the figure of Bacchus in the flower-filled embrasure behind him. It was a good setting for him.

He's seventy-six with soft white hair, a plump, banker's face and impeccable tailoring. He looks no more than sixty. There's an air of sincerity about him that is completely misleading – unless you can describe a wolf as having sincerity. His head was bent and he was reading an evening newspaper, his spectacles lodged half-way down his nose so that he could longsight the bar without changing position. The only other person in the room was the barman. I bought myself a scotch on the rocks and carried it to the Bishop's table. He lowered his newspaper very slowly as I pulled a chair and sat down. It took him about thirty seconds to paste a smile over shocked incredulity.

'For God's sake!' he exclaimed. 'If it isn't the original Rover Boy!'

His accent is a mixture of his native Canadian and acquired British vowel-sounds. The world may have passed him by but he has retained his resiliency. I put my glass down carefully, taking in the white Sulka shirt, handmade shoes and blue hopsack suit. The old rogue is an actor and his clothes are his props. His very existence depends on his good appearance.

'How are you?' I asked politely. 'Still managing to find those marks with larceny in their hearts?'

Pain clouded his face. 'I've had the goddam gout,' he

84

observed, looking down at his right foot.

I nodded sympathetically. 'It's the high-living. That and your aristocratic blood.' There's a saying that's gone the rounds. If you shake hands with the Bishop it's advisable to count your fingers afterwards.

He removed his spectacles and looked indignant.

'What the hell's that supposed to mean?' he demanded. 'What are you, some kind of comedian?' He mimicked my voice. '"That and your aristocratic blood!"'

I took a sip of the malt. 'I'm only checking. I like to keep up with old friends.'

'Bullshit!' he said mistrustfully. 'What's on your mind?'

'Well,' I said, stretching out my legs. 'As a matter of fact I need your help.'

He winced visibly. 'I don't like the sound of that. I don't like the sound of that at all.'

'I didn't expect you would. But you owe me one, Bishop. Cast your mind back and think about it for a while.'

There are scoundrels you can't help having a sneaking regard for. The Bishop is one of them, one of the last of a vanishing species. The old-style conmen have gone, their world taken over by less colourful swindlers. The Bishop had survived by lowering his sights and putting the bite on visiting foreigners. It was a safe enough gambit since the amounts involved were never sufficiently large for the victims to complain to the police. All of them had to return to their homelands and what the Bishop did was simply avoid the places where he made his scores. Yet once he had been the best of his time, conning the rich, the greedy and the gullible. At

85

the age of seventy-six I suppose he ought to have been in a home for the aged. But I was somehow glad that he wasn't.

'O.K., I've thought about it,' he said, lifting his head. 'What kind of help do you need? I haven't turned a trick in weeks and I'm two months behind with my rent.'

A couple of the American women came into the room and headed for the bar. They ordered martinis. The Spanish barman listened to their instructions with supercilious attention. I kept my voice low.

'I want an address. The Ratcatcher's.'

He covered his nose with his hand, muttering through his fingers. 'I think we're getting into a misunderstanding here, Raven. You know goddam well that I don't associate with hoodlums.'

That much was true. Our acquaintanceship went back ten years to an awkward time for my venerable companion. He'd been on the fringe of a caper involving a hundred thousand pounds' worth of stolen travellers' cheques. It was my case and I'd run it from London to Paris and back coming up with only one name, the Bishop's. I'd known that he wasn't the man I really wanted and ran him to earth in the Carlton Towers, staying under the style of Gustave Prentiss, mining-engineer. I'd offered him a deal. He was too old even then to spend the rest of his life in jail so he gave me the two Shashoua brothers and a handsome conviction. No one else ever knew about our arrangement and his reputation as an Elder Statesman of Crime remained intact. I never asked him to open his mouth again. The Bishop had a fine contempt for violent crime. Like the rest of his school, he had stolen his money with flimflam and smiles rather than with a sawn-off shotgun.

'You could find out for me,' I suggested.

He folded his arms like a preacher faced with an immodest proposal. 'You've known me since I first came to this country, Raven. I'm an old man but apart from this goddam gout I'm reasonably healthy. And that's the way I want to stay.'

The American women were still discussing their drinks with the barman. I slipped a couple of ten pound notes under the Bishop's newspaper.

'Nobody'll know a thing,' I urged. 'If it hadn't been for me you'd have been on the Moor, walking round those concrete circles. In a cell with your own little transistor. Chapel on Sunday, cottage-pie and cocoa. You'd have died in there, Bishop.'

He crossed his fingers and shuddered but made no move to touch the money.

'What do you want with this bum anyway?'

I emptied the last of my drink. 'I'm starting a string-quartet and I hear he plays fiddle.'

He wagged his head slowly. 'I can't make up my mind about you.'

I closed one eye. 'The Shashouas did. They thought I was just another cop who got lucky.'

He moved his untouched vermouth. 'Why did they knock you off the force, Raven? There's a rumour that you were bent.'

'I heard it,' I answered. The note of criticism in his voice was a reminder that I'd lost credit with people like him as well as with my ex-colleagues. 'There are twenty pounds under that newspaper. That's all it's worth so put it in your pocket and start doing some telephoning.'

He pushed the money back across the table, looking at me with blue eyes that were younger than the rest of his face. Suddenly he got to his feet.

'Either I owe you one or I don't. Better get yourself another drink. This could take some time.'

It was half-an-hour before he came back. He sat down heavily. 'I just remembered something you once said to me. "In my job you do what you have to do." I guess it's the same for everybody.'

' "The protection of law and property." That's what it says in the instruction book for Metropolitan police officers. It isn't quite the same thing as you have in mind. Did you get what I want?'

He parted with the information reluctantly. 'This is hearsay but it's good hearsay. Number ten Swallow Street, Paddington. If he's not there the word is that he spends a lot of time in the Garden of Jade. I'm told it's a massage-parlour just around the corner.'

I memorised the addresses and nodded my thanks. 'You've been a big help, Bishop. Drink up and have one on me before I go.'

He grimaced, flexing his foot. 'No more for me. As far as I'm concerned we're quits, Raven. Do me a favour and don't come back.'

'Relax,' I said. 'I'm the soul of discretion.'

As far as I knew he had no family. Someone once said that there are only two ways of growing old. One is to be loved, the other is to be rich. Whoever did say it was forgetting the quality of endurance, the quality that enables an old rascal like the Bishop to survive out of time and context.

'If I ever live to be your age I hope I do as well,' I said sincerely.

'You won't.' The thought seemed to give him pleasure. 'Not the way you're going. You're too goddam certain that you're right all the time and I have my own thought about that. You're a loser, Raven. One of these guys born with a perverse will to lose. That's what makes you do these crazy things.'

I couldn't help laughing. 'That just about does it. I've heard you banging on about the plight of the stock market and the future of Charolais breeding but this is the first time you've surveyed the field of psychiatry.'

For some reason or other the remark seemed to needle him. He eyed the distance from our table to the women at the bar and lowered his voice.

'Why don't you just fuck off, Raven? Who do you think you are, for Crissakes – some kind of avenging angel? You can't accept the fact that you're not a cop any longer. It's a sickness with you.'

I took my car keys and stood up. 'I'll see you, Bishop. Take care.'

He shook out his newspaper and adjusted his spectacles. 'What the hell, you know it all anyway. Goodbye, Raven.'

'Look after yourself,' I said and I meant it. I left the hotel with a knot of excitement in my stomach.

I made my way to Piccadilly looking for a free phone. I had to go down to the Underground station to find one. There was the usual parade of riffraff mingling with the bona-fide passengers. Teenage hustlers, vicious and insolent, loitered near the men's lavatory. Pill-pedlars moved furtively from exit to exit searching for their contacts. They give themselves fixes on the staircases, trip in the w.c.s and pass out in their own vomit. There's usually one of their own kind there to drag them away.

The occasional police patrol passes but there seems to be little that they can do. They pick off the odd straggler from the herd, some dull-eyed youth or a girl who is obviously under age. A couple of months afterwards they're back again.

A sign of the time was Arabic graffiti adorning the walls of the phone-box. I called Jerry Soo's number and this time he answered.

'It's me,' I announced. 'Is Louise with you?'

'Louise is in Bristol doing a concert. Why?'

The highrise block he lives in is built on the site of an old paper warehouse. His windows were open and I could hear the sounds of the river in the background. The uproar of the city had gone.

'I have to see you right away. It's not the sort of thing to explain on the phone but it's urgent.'

'That's O.K.,' he said easily, sounding like Granite-Jaw Granger in some storm-buffeted control tower talking down the pilot whose nerve has gone. 'Where are you speaking from?'

'Piccadilly Underground Station. Can you come to the boat right away?'

'You're not in any sort of trouble, are you?' he asked quickly. 'I mean, I heard Drake was at that inquest.'

'I don't know what I'm in,' I said truthfully. 'But it's big and it's probably dangerous.'

'Hankypanky,' he said. 'I see. I'll be there as soon as I can.'

The phone-box stank of unwashed bodies. I opened the door with my toe. The thought of seeing him made me feel better.

'I'll wait outside the pub for you.'

I hung up and tried Teresa's number again. There

was no reply. My hunch was that Olga's boyfriend had moved her on somewhere. There was one person who obviously knew what had happened but I couldn't very well go calling on Kirstie Melinda MacDonald. I drove back to Chelsea by way of the river, the fishbowl street lamps strung along the Embankment illuminating the glassy pavements. Lights traced the spans of five bridges and Battersea power station was a fortress with pink-washed turrets. I parked outside the Mariners Rest and smoked cigarettes nervously until Jerry Soo's souped-up Mini streaked out of the rain. He braked, going into a controlled skid that brought him alongside the Citroën. He climbed into the seat beside me.

'I'm sorry if I'm late. There's a burst sewer at Battersea and the road is up.'

He was wearing his usual off-duty outfit, a blue-quilted anorak, drainpipe trousers and soft black leather boots that he has made in Hong Kong. I've always suspected that someone must have stretched him before he took his medical on induction. He's barely the minimum height required for the Metropolitan Police and most of his weight is in his shoulders. His scalp shows blue through a bristle of black hair and his eyes are like shiny boot-buttons. His face is stretched tightly from one cheekbone to another, the skin looking as if it has been waxed and then polished. Jerry smiles all the time, even when he's asleep. I've been on a couple of fishing holidays with him in Norway, deep in the fjords, our sleeping-bags under the fir trees. I've watched him dead to the world, lying with a bland smile on his face. It's a polite, self-effacing smile that hides explosive physical power. Jerry was the star of the Metropolitan Judo team, wrestling men who were twenty and thirty pounds heavier.

'You look good,' he said approvingly. 'Muscles under the eyes and a magnificent hair development. You must be eating regularly.'

'Riveting,' I said. 'An astonishing sense of humour.'

The way Jerry tells the story he was found in a fish-basket on the steps of the Shanghai and Hong Kong Banking Corporation, about three weeks old and suffering from malnutrition and an extreme case of jaundice. A policeman took the basket to the Moravian Mission Hospital where its occupant was christened Gerald Lee Soo. Gerald was for the doctor who supervised the infant's change of blood, Lee and Soo for two of the Chinese nurses. The approximate date of birth was entered as 8 February, nineteen-thirty-six. People in the hospital must have taken a liking to him because the place was to be his home for the next sixteen years.

It was Friday night and the pub was getting rowdy.

'Let's get out of here,' I suggested. 'We'll talk on the boat.'

He sat in my rocking-chair, watching silently as I put on a record. There are things about me that he has come to accept without comment. One of them is my compulsive need to walk or listen to music in times of stress. There are other things that he accepts without approving. Most of all what he calls my 'shark-obstinacy'. It seems that sharks in his part of the world are obstinate.

I turned down the volume, letting the sound of rain mingle with Chopin. I poured him a glass of the Pernod he loves and gave myself a scotch. Drink wasn't going to affect my reasoning. My brain was way ahead of alcohol. Jerry added ice to his glass, pursing his lips judiciously as the liquid clouded.

'You want to hear a funny story?' I asked.

He sipped his Pernod, boot-button eyes considering me. 'I like funny stories.'

I took him through the events of the day, omitting nothing. His jaw-muscles bulged.

'I'd say that this has all the makings of an intriguing situation.'

Sitting as we were, insulated from the outside world, we might have done as we often did, get out the chessboard and forget time. But it wasn't going to be like that.

'Is that the best you can do?' I asked quietly.

He rid himself of his anorak. Underneath was a T-shirt with a Mickey Mouse emblem emblazoned across the chest.

'You haven't told me what you expect,' he answered mildly.

That much was easy. 'I expect you to help me.'

'Help you do what? All this moralising is out-of-character, John. I mean this indignation at the thought of someone taking advantage of an innocent maiden. It doesn't ring true. I suspect that what you really want to do is stick one in Drake's eye. Isn't that it?'

I had to smile. 'That's it,' I admitted. I don't always like what Jerry says but it has the effect of making me be honest with myself. 'It's been more than eighteen months and the bastard still won't get off my back.'

He looked at me serenely, his face as old as the Great Wall of China. 'It's more than that, isn't it, John?'

I lifted a shoulder. 'O.K., it's more than just that. I may not be a cop any longer but the feelings are still there. If I walked away from this one now I'd feel that I'd been defrauded.'

He stuffed a piece of ginseng root in his mouth. He claims that chewing the stuff is good for brain, wind and bowels.

'It was Drake who put that rumour about, but you'll never be able to prove it.'

The record came to a stop. I switched off the machine. 'Maybe not but if I sewed this thing up I could knock his eye out. Don't forget that Jack Armstrong is still with Window on the World.' The television producer was a small dusty man who owed me a favour from the Zaleski case.

Jerry champed the aromatic root. 'Ex-Scotland Yard detective nails notorious villain. I like it.'

'It could work,' I urged. 'And that's where you come in, Jerry. I want to give this whole thing to the right sort of cop. Someone who isn't scared of the establishment. And I want to be taken along for the ride.'

He sank lower in the rocking-chair, left cheek bulging. He chewed vigorously, his gaze on the ceiling. His foot stopped the rocking suddenly.

'Someone with enough clout to be able to walk into the Commissioner's office if he has to? Someone who's snotty and ambitious and above all someone who dislikes Drake?'

'Right,' I said cautiously.

He sat up straight, grinning like a mantelpiece Buddha. 'You want Joe Mallory. He made an application to join A10 and Drake turned him down. He's still on the Flying Squad.'

The name meant nothing to me but there was no reason why it should. The composition of the Flying

Squad changes constantly. It's the easiest place in the world to get a medal or a black eye. The joke used to be that if you made the Squad and didn't get an arrest within twenty-four hours you were back on the beat trying to work out who burgled Cohen's Beigel Bakery.

'Do you know this Mallory personally?'

He held the rocking-chair steady with his small dapper feet. 'Let's put it this way. I know him better than he knows me. He's straight but he's hungry. And he's not above cutting corners if he thinks it's in his favour. No, he's your man, John. All we have to do is convince him of it.'

I worried a cigarette from the pack. 'What's it going to take, for Crissakes. I'm offering him one of the biggest villains in the country on a plate.'

He scratched through short black hair, shutting his eyes like a stroked cat.

'It's a good one, all right. I'd say it should add up to ten for the Ratcatcher and a commendation for Mallory. He ought to go for it. If there's any doubt at all it's that he may think you're asking too much.'

'Too much?' I retorted. 'All I'm asking is to be in at the death so that I can go on Armstrong's programme and talk about it. And if *that's* out-of-character, I couldn't care less. It's what I want.'

He stretched his arms. 'We can but try. Is your phone clean?'

I looked at him sharply. He appeared to be serious. 'I mean it,' he said. 'This stuff's dynamite and you never know.'

He had a point. Over twenty thousand telephones are supposed to be bugged in the Metropolitan area of London alone. It isn't just the police who are doing it. It's the intelligence branches of outfits like Customs and Excise, the Internal Revenue Service, MI5 and MI6. If you add to these the hundreds of private-inquiry agents, 'research-consultants' and industrial spies, you begin to get some idea of the threat posed. Unauthorised bugging is denied but it exists.

'Help yourself,' I invited.

He dialled three digits and followed with my number. A metallic voice sounded in the earpiece.

'Stark Test. Stark Test. Stark Test.'

He put the phone down, his lips moving as he counted to five. The phone rang. He lifted and replaced the receiver.

'You're clean.'

The way it works is simple. A phone can only handle one recording device at a time. Jerry had just dialled the code signal used by Post Office engineers testing a faulty line. The fact that the recorded voice answered meant that my phone wasn't bugged. I went into the bedroom and collected a sample of Bertorelli's burglary-kit. Jerry was chatting away in the sitting room. By the time I rejoined him he had finished his conversation and was standing at the window, staring down river.

'So?' I demanded.

He swung round. 'He's out on a job. I had to go through Mobile. He's interested all right.'

Something in his voice intrigued me. 'What's that supposed to mean?'

He showed me all his teeth. 'He gave the Ratcatcher a pull a couple of weeks ago. Burns was clean and didn't like it. Said he was being harassed, a man trying to go straight. He threatened to complain to his member of parliament.'

I switched off the kitchen lights. 'What exactly did you tell Mallory?'

'All he needed to know,' he answered. 'He's driving to Kensington Square and waiting there for us. It's out-of-the-way and quiet. You can tell him the rest yourself.'

I nodded. 'There's one thing I'm not quite clear about. You keep saying "we" and "us". You've got no right to be mixed up in any of this.'

His grin grew wider, his blackcurrant eyes almost disappearing. 'It's my weekend off, right? I was having a drink with a friend and we ran into a fellow-officer who asked for assistance. How could I refuse?'

'You're nuts,' I said. There was nobody I'd sooner have had by my side but I could hardly tell him that.

CHAPTER SEVEN

We took the two cars, Jerry leading the way in his Mini.
He drives as he does most things, with care, courtesy
and decision. I followed the flashing indicators down
Thackeray Street into Kensington Square. He stopped
outside the convent. Lighted windows studded the
façades of the tall elegant houses. Rain dripped on the
bushes and grass beyond the railings. Flying Squad cars
are no longer recognisable. Gone are the days of
bloomed-glass back windows and the telltale central
radio-mast. An unmarked Jaguar was drawn up on the
north side of the square. The driver opened the rear
door for us and the interior light came on. Mallory was
built like a footballer with shave-scraped cheeks and a
nose like a pear sliced in half. His velour hat had a
feather in the band and he was wearing a green loden-
cloth cape. Jerry made the introductions. Mallory gave
me a hand, his appraisal sharp under ginger eyebrows.
His accent was cockney.

'Pleased to meet you. I know who you are. I made it
my business as soon as Jerry called.'

His directness gave me confidence. 'And did you hear
that I was bent?'

'I heard,' he said. 'But I didn't listen. I happen to
know the Commander.'

'As long as we know how we stand. You get the Ratcatcher and I get a slot on television. The Commander
won't be pleased with either.'

He rested his back against the door, considering me carefully. 'That's all right with me,' he said after a while. 'If your story's right you can write your own ticket.'

A bell tolled in the convent chapel, the sound muffled in the wet darkness. It was twenty to eight by the clock on the dash. Something spurred a sudden doubt in me, a fear that the Ratcatcher would give us the slip.

'It has to be like that,' I said.

'Within limits,' he answered. 'You know the game as well as I do. There are certain things that you can't do. You're not on the strength any longer.'

'Fuck the strength,' I said deliberately. 'And fuck what's reasonable. I'm going to stand in front of those television cameras and make some controversial statements about the abuse of power and privilege within the Metropolitan Police Authority.'

Mallory glanced at Jerry who just shook his head and went on smiling. 'You mean you're going to mention Drake?' demanded Mallory.

'That's exactly what I mean.'

He made a sound like a sheep bleating. 'That'll be one programme that I don't intend to miss. O.K., let's get down to business. Do you know where the Ratcatcher is? C.R.O.'s a dead loss. All they can say is that he was released from the Moor in September.'

'I've got an address and I'm checking it out,' I admitted.

I expected an objection but he let the answer ride. 'What about this other joker, the dead girl's boyfriend. Have you any idea who he is?'

'I've seen him,' I said. 'I'm almost sure that he went back to Tregunter Road and picked up the Venezuelan girl. If I'm right she's in danger.' I gave him the registration of the Ford Capri. Mallory used the radiophone for a check on the car's ownership.

'Do you think the girl could be part of it?' he asked.

I shook my head. 'All she did was a favour for a friend and it backfired. Nothing more than that.'

We talked for a couple of minutes and the phone buzzed. Mallory listened, making a face. He put the receiver down again.

'That car belongs to the Duke Hire Company at London Airport. The man who rented it this morning left a cash deposit and showed an International driving licence in the name of Roland Berry. He said he'd be touring for a few days and gave his address as care of Thomas Cook, Berkeley Street. We can have him pulled if you like.'

'Let it go,' I said. 'At least till I've checked this address. He isn't going to be driving the girl around now. They'll be holed-up somewhere.'

He looked as his watch. 'O.K. There's something that I have to do in any case. It shouldn't take more than an hour. Where are you people going to be?'

I pointed at the radiophone. 'Can I reach you on that or not?'

He nodded. 'Ring Mobile and ask for Freddy Sergeant one-two-three. Do you think you'll have something by then?'

'I'll have something,' I promised.

He reached behind and unfastened the door. 'Be lucky!'

Jerry and I hurried back to the Citroën. He climbed in beside me, wiping the rain from his face with the sleeve of his anorak.

'What do you think?'

I threw my poncho on the back seat. 'I'm not sure. I mean I'm not sure about his discretion. The Ratcatcher's no fool, remember. I don't want Mallory charging in, head down and swinging.'

He used a match to dislodge a piece of ginseng from a back tooth.

'He'll do whatever he says, John. No more, no less. That's the way he's made. I suppose you want to go to Paddington on your own?'

Girls were going into the convent chapel. There was a glimpse of candles on an altar beyond the open door, a whiff of incense.

'That's right. I want to go on my own. You try Tregunter Road again. Ring some of the doorbells. Say you're a friend of Teresa's. Or say you're from the language school. That's even better.'

He went into his chopsuey accent. 'Hurro Saror! You think I look like someone from a language school?'

'You look what you are,' I said. 'A wily bloody oriental.'

His voice lost its banter. 'You've got an idea about Burns?'

'Sure,' I said. 'He's going to blow a safe. There are something like five thousand banks in the Greater London area. Add a couple of hundred safety-deposit vaults, travel agencies with banking facilities, jewellery stores, numismatists and diamond-brokers. You take your pick.'

It was an act of faith that the Ratcatcher wasn't going to make his move until I'd had the chance to locate him. Once I'd done that, the rest would be easy. Police methods have become more sophisticated. The leap-frog method of tailing a suspect's car is literally foolproof. Radio-directed vehicles of all types take up the chase, overlapping one another.

Jerry zipped up his anorak. 'Where do we meet?'

I gave him the name of a pub near Paddington Station. Whoever got there first would wait for the other. Once together we could call Mallory. I watched the tail-lights glow as the Mini braked at the corner. The address the Bishop had given me was close to Norfolk Square. No matter what the country, the neighbourhood surrounding large railway stations always seems to be sleazy. Paddington is no exception. There's a square mile of cheap eating places, discount houses selling electronic equipment, purveyors of trusses and surgical equipment, pawnshops, secondhand clothing stores, locksmiths, dental repair parlours and the ubiquitous sex shops. I left the Citröen in front of a rundown boarding house describing itself as the Eton Hall Hotel, Vacancies, No Singles. A man emerged from the shadows as I neared the corner. He was carrying a sandwich-board bearing the legend

PROTEIN EQUALS LUST
LESS PROTEIN LESS LUST

I wrapped myself in my poncho and walked on past dubious-looking restaurants and gift shops filled with rubbish. Black faces with enormous whites of eyes peered from doorways, Arab women passed, their eyes and noses veiled. The pub where Jerry and I were to meet was a mock-Tudor tavern where people jostled one another in front of a blaring jukebox. I located the phone on the stairs and went outside again. Swallow Street ran left and right immediately in front of me. It was a cut above its neighbours and reasonably well-lit. There are similar streets all over London, legacies from the last century. Streets of what were once called 'artisans' dwellings', three up and three down with outside lavatories. Some of the houses had been converted, with fake Queen Anne windows and doors. Number ten was in its original state, a dirty-jowled house with paint peeling on the woodwork and a decided lurch forward. A plastic dustbin stood outside the front door. I walked past rapidly, looking straight ahead. I had the impression that the entire house was in darkness. I turned at the end of the street and came back as far as the grocer's on the corner.

It was a dingy building with the sign *Cassidy's Family Grocery* painted above the entrance. The shop windows were filled with a haphazard assemblage of washing-powder, canned fruit, tights, chocolate, candles and soap. The glass case on the wall outside advertised a variety of special services. I read the details, watching the reflection of the Ratcatcher's house in the glass.

> Arts and Crafts for the Connoisseur
> Young Lady Seeks Driving Post
> Corrective training by Miss Bond
> Large chest for sale

Each card bore a telephone number. The way the window was set made it difficult for me to see the whole of the house I was watching. I opened the door to the store and a bell tinkled. The Pakistani couple behind the counter were trying to deal with an elderly woman in hair-curlers. She was pointing at a refrigerated shelf, her voice querulous.

'Cheese! *Cheddar*, dear!'

The Pakistani's worried face cleared and he took on stature, snapping his fingers at his wife.

'Cheesery Cheddery!' he said triumphantly. He turned towards me, clearly pleased with himself. 'Yes please?'

I pointed at the shelf of cigarettes. I could see the house now through the other window. There wasn't a light on the front of the building.

'Which one please?' He was standing on tiptoe at the same time trying to oversee his wife's performance with the cheese.

I paid and stepped out into the drizzle. A dark desolate street of condemned houses ran parallel to Swallow Street. The windows were boarded-up, the doors covered with sheets of galvanized iron to discourage the incursion of squatters. A series of well-aimed rocks had put the street lamps out of commission. I found a telephone box and asked the operator for the Swallow Street number. It rang for five minutes unanswered. I returned to the row of condemned houses and climbed a crumbling brick wall. I dropped into a yard with perilous rusting bicycles and broken milk bottles. I climbed another wall with more difficulty and landed on cinders in the back yard of number ten. A dog started to bark loudly. I flattened myself against the rough brick wall. I could hear a child crying somewhere, the distant sound of Edgware Road traffic, half-a-dozen television sets offering the same programme.

I moved from cinders on to muddy earth, the soles of my shoes squelching as I eased forward cautiously. The dog had stopped barking.

It wouldn't be the first time that I'd burgled a house.

Don't believe the cop who says that he never breaks the law. I slipped on a pair of leather gloves. The back door resisted my pressure, bolted both top and bottom. The frames of the kitchen windows were secured with screw-type bolts. A window above was open but the plastic drainpipe would never have held my weight. I made my way round to the front of the house again. The pavement stretched, deserted under the lamplight. I stood in the doorway of number ten, rain dripping inside the neck of my poncho. I make no claims to being a cracksman. I just happened to be carrying a superb set of burglary equipment. The third key I tried turned the mortise lock leaving the door secured by a spring lock. A woman's silhouette showed behind the grille-protected windows next door. I used a master key on the spring-lock and stood in the dark hallway listening to a cistern being flushed upstairs. Pipes clanked in the wall cavity and I realised that the noises came from the neighbouring house.

There was a musty smell compounded of airless rooms and greasy food, the smell Cathy used to describe as 'poverty'. I wiped my feet thoroughly on the doormat so that I made no tracks on the linoleum. The street lamp outside laid a shaft of light across the shabbily-furnished front room with its cheap prints hung on mustard-coloured walls. Small noises echoed through the empty house. Rafters creaked and a refrigerator motor whirred. I tiptoed down a passage to the kitchen, shielding the flame of my lighter with cupped hand. The kettle on the gas-cooker was cold. The only provisions I could see were milk in the refrigerator, tea and sugar. A vase on the mantel contained a receipted bill for a month's rent paid in advance. The name of the lessee was Allen. I reasoned that if I could hear the people next door they could hear me. For all I knew they could be friends of the Ratcatcher's. I went up the stairs keeping close to the wall.

One of the three rooms on the second storey was completely empty. I took my shielded light into the front bedroom. The single bed was made and covered with a padded quilt. There was a telephone on a nearby table and an open copy of a girlie magazine. The cheap chest-of-drawers and wardrobe were empty except for clothes hangers. I moved to the other bedroom. The quilt was disarranged as if someone had been lying on the bed. I still believed that the Bishop had given me the right information but as yet I'd seen nothing to prove it, nothing to suggest that the Ratcatcher occupied the house. Net curtains billowed in the half-open window, rain pattering softly against the panes. Something lifted on the floor, caught in the current of air. Something white. I bent and retrieved the scrap of paper. It was a message from the *concierge* at the *Baur au Lac* hotel in Zürich.

Swissair confirms your flight to London tomorrow.

The message was timed nineteen-forty hours on the previous day. Adrenalin boosted my pulse-rate. Olga's boyfriend *had* been here. And if he'd been here then so had the Ratcatcher. I bent down, sniffing at the pillow. I recognised the scent Teresa Cintron had been wearing that morning. My hunch must have been right. Once the Ratcatcher knew how much into things Teresa was he had made up his mind to grab her. The fair-haired man must have doubled back to Tregunter Road, conned Teresa into accompanying him and brought her here. What came next I preferred not to think about.

The Ratcatcher was a pro. When the time came to vacate the house he would leave no fingerprints, nothing that would identify him. He might well make sure that his partner went through the same procedures. I dropped the slip of paper on the floor where I'd found it and hurried down the stairs. I let myself out through the front door, shutting it gently behind me.

It was five minutes to nine. The Pakistanis in the corner shop were putting up the shutters. I was feeling robbed and defeated, wondering whether it wouldn't have been better to stay with the man in the Ford Capri instead of the Ratcatcher. I had a feeling that he was as good a lead to the imminent robbery. I trotted back to the pub. The saloon bar was even louder and smokier but I couldn't see Jerry. The massage parlour the Bishop had spoken of was no more than a couple of hundred yards away in Sussex Mews. I went into the men's room and did what I could to make myself look presentable.

Coloured lights ran over the entrance to the *Garden of Jade* creating strange shapes in green and fiery red. I pushed the door open. The air-arm closed it for me gently. I was in a room hung with blown-up photographs of men lying on their backs attended by girls dressed in some sort of oriental costume. Both the men and the women had their faces screwed into expressions of sly abandon. Magazines featuring female nudes were scattered around on a low opium-table where joss-sticks were burning. Aromatic smoke curled against a long oval mirror and the carpet was like soft turf. Tinkling music was coming from hidden speakers. There was an open appointment-book on a desk but I was unable to read the entries upside down. An opaque glass door at the end of the room led to what I took to be the functional part of the establishment. I had an idea that the glass was one-way vision and cleared my throat noisily.

The door opened as if on cue. A woman with Chinese features glided in, showing goldfilled teeth. She was wearing trousers and smock of matching silk and her hair was skewered with an ivory pin. She was at least ten years older than I was and a great deal surer of herself. Her singsong voice was childish, her smile suggestive.

'Good evening, sir. What can I do for you?'

The glass door was half-open and I could see the frosted panels of the sauna cubicles. A woman laughed. There was something about the place that weakened my certainty. If the Ratcatcher was here I wasn't worried about him seeing me. He'd never laid eyes on me in his life. But the more I thought about it, the less likely it seemed that he *would* be here.

I gave her the sort of look that I hoped she'd interpret as embarrassment.

'It's about the massage, really. I was wondering how it went. I mean about the charges and things.'

Her gaze flicked over me, assessing the poncho, jeans and generally scruffy appearance.

'Massage and sauna-bath coming together. No one without the other. Half-hour session costing twelve pounds. Service charge extra.'

I whistled softly. She closed the glass door with enough emphasis to reprimand my curiosity.

'That seems a little steep,' I suggested. 'I mean twelve pounds for just a sauna bath.'

'Silly, silly,' she reproved indulgently. 'What your name?'

'Smith,' I said, poker-faced.

She nodded. 'Mistuh Smith. You staying here, nice pretty girls. They making big fuss of you. So I make cubicle ready, yes?'

I turned my wrist, looking at my watch. 'Another time, maybe. Goodnight.'

She went on smiling as I shut the door hurriedly, sealing in her musky scent and the tinkling music. The wet air outside was pleasantly refreshing. I filled my lungs with it and strode out briskly. The old coach-houses had been converted into workshops and garages, premises that were unoccupied from six o'clock at night until eight the following morning. During the weekends there was nobody there. The space between the door-ways was piled high with refuse of all kinds, sacks stuffed with sawdust, empty cartons and plywood offcuts. As I neared the end of the mews, I heard the slither of leather soles close behind me and turned, defending my head with my arm instinctively. The Ratcatcher swung a cloth-wrapped pickaxe shaft viciously, getting me on the left shoulder. My arm dropped, pain numbing my muscles. He swung again, this time aiming a little higher. The blow took me on the side of the head. My brain seemed to explode in a coruscation of stars and I knew I was falling. I felt my hands and knees skid across the greasy cobblestones and then everything was black and still.

CHAPTER EIGHT

I came to my senses spluttering. My hair, face and clothes
were soaked with water. Gradually my eyes began to
focus, taking in the checked tablecloth and the stained
refrigerator. I was lying on the floor of number ten
Swallow Street. The curtains had been pulled across the
kitchen windows and the receipted bill had been removed from the vase on the mantel. The Ratcatcher
put the empty jug back in the sink and leaned against
the wall. He was dressed in a respectable suit with a
tie, his pale flat hair as lank as a curate's, his eyes cold
above the hare's mouth. He motioned me up with the
snubnosed pistol in his right hand. A large negro in
chauffeur's livery filled the kitchen doorway. He grinned
happily as I rose, fingering the eggshaped lump above
my left ear. My legs went suddenly and I grabbed at
the table. The Ratcatcher's hand moved threateningly.
I pushed my arms at the ceiling.

'Take a guid look at this one, Trinny,' he said with
hostile eyes. 'You'll no see the like every day. This one
was Detective-Inspector Raven.'

The negro wagged his head in mute wonder. 'Ow!'
he said.

'Aye,' said the Ratcatcher. 'Ask him what he's doing
here, Trinny.'

The negro's grin faded. 'Why you bothering respectable workingmen, man?'

I stood perfectly still, wondering where Jerry could be. I was fairly sure that I'd given him this address. The problem was whether or not he'd remember it.

The Ratcatcher moved off the wall, the cylinder of the revolver shifting under the pressure of his finger.

'You know who I am?'

I nodded. The gesture seemed to afford him satisfaction. I wet my dry lips.

'You're making a mistake. I'm on your side. I came here to help you.'

For a moment I thought he'd choke. A Y-shaped vein stood out on his forehead and his voice was shaky. He was cunning and vicious but too uncontrolled to be really big time. He finally got a hold on himself.

'One wrong move, ye wee bastard and I'll give ye another hole to fart with!'

He jammed the pistol into my side. The negro went through the hall and opened the street door. Rain hissed on the empty pavements and I thought of Mallory waiting for our call. A large Daimler limousine was drawn up outside. The negro donned a chauffeur's cap and took the wheel. The Ratcatcher glanced left and right then shoved me forward. I sat behind Trinny, the Ratcatcher next to me.

'Home, James,' he said. 'And dinna spare the horses.'

A knife-scar seamed the negro's neck. Had the circle been completed the cut must have taken his head off. I was still in a state of some shock but I was now noticing things. The revolver sitting in the Ratcatcher's lap was a Smith and Wesson thirty-eight with a two-inch barrel. And his hands were jumpy. The limousine surged forward, turning left from Edgware Road into Marylebone. The rain had gathered momentum and was bouncing off the tops of the bus-shelters. Traffic was heavy in spite of the miserable weather. The lights held us at Euston. Blank faces of bus passengers stared back disinterestedly. Every stop was an invitation to make a run for it but I knew that I'd never make the kerb. I kept my eye on the rearview mirror, hoping for some sign of help. I'd no idea what had happened to Jerry. The Bishop's face kept floating into my consciousness, smiling benevolently. It was obvious that he'd set me up. Burns must have missed me at his house but going to the *Garden of Jade* I had to use the mews. Trinny and the Ratcatcher had simply waited there for me. It was strange the way I had misjudged the Bishop. I'd gambled on the fact that I'd saved him from going to jail. So he owed me a favour. Looking back I could see the fallacy in the reasoning. What I had done was turn him into a stool-pigeon and he had never forgiven me for it.

The Ratcatcher's head snapped sideways as I felt in my pocket. I showed him the lighter and cigarettes in my hand. No cop ever won a popularity contest but the Ratcatcher's was more than just professional dislike, it was pure malevolence. I lit a smoke and leaned back. As I did so I smelled the familiar odour. There was gelignite in the back of the car.

Burns's harelipped smile was supercilious. 'Aye, ye always did like your wee grasses, didn't ye, Raven. Well, I've a message for ye. The Bishop says that a man who'll blow the whistle on his own kind is nae to be trusted.'

We were speeding along Commercial Road, with its network of squalid streets, its garish pubs and jellied-eel stands under soaked awnings. It was a neighbourhood of cheap villainy where forlorn hustlers waited for visiting sailors. A forest of crane-jibs rose above the grey anonymous streets. Angry red lights hung high in the sky above the clatter of chains and donkey-engines. We were entering the web of canals, bridges and waterways that cling to the north bank of the Thames. Weirs, sluices and locks tame and divert the river. Spring brings blossom to hedged lanes completely ignored on the architects' drawingboards, lanes that meander past pubs once used by smugglers, ocean-going ships moored close to graveyards. It's a strange scene unlike any other part of the world. I sneaked a look at the speedometer. We'd covered nine miles since leaving Swallow Street. A sign pointed the way to the Royal docks. Trinny turned the Daimler in the opposite direction, towards the Barking bypass. The rain rushed at the headlamps as we swung on to a narrow road that followed the curves in the river. There was no other traffic here, no street or house lights, nothing but a flat expanse of mud. The surface of the road was holed and damaged. Trinny dropped to a lower gear, the motor whining. The river was twenty feet on our right, marked by a sagging fence. The glow ahead became floodlights illuminating a red-brick powerhouse. A driveway led to the entrance where a couple of guards were standing out of the rain beneath a portico. One of them was holding a leashed Doberman. Trinny stopped the car and switched off the lights. When you sit in the dark with a couple of villains your brain isn't exactly analytical. I found myself wondering whether I hadn't come at this from the wrong angle. The line was blurred between crime and terrorism. Anarchists and the so-called soldiers of the I.R.A. robbed and murdered. Suppose the Ratcatcher were mixed up in politics. He might well be going to blow up the power-station.

We sat silent in the car till the guard with the dog headed into the rain towards the buildings behind. His colleague closed the door of the gatehouse. Trinny re-started the motor. We whispered past the driveway, down a muddy track to a derelict pier. The river was a half-mile wide at this point, a choppy expanse of dark water dotted with the lights of moored vessels. A deso-late stand of abandoned warehouses stretched along the north bank, the rotting timber and broken windows monuments to a trade with a bygone empire. The Rat-catcher leaned across and unfastened the door. He dug the gun in my ribs.

'Out!'

Trinny made no move to follow us. I stepped on to slippery planks. High tide had brought the smell of salt water. The Ratcatcher was close behind as I walked along the pier. The uprights had sunk over the years and the end of the pier was submerged. There was a sense of unreality about what was happening to me. The water was deep on both sides and I suppose I could have gone in but Burns would have put a bullet in me long before I hit the surface. His voice brought me to a halt. The beam from the flashlight in his hand settled on a dinghy that was nuzzling the green slimy timber. He shifted the beam, indicating the seat in the bows. I climbed down awkwardly, the dinghy rocking under my weight. The Ratcatcher followed, casting-off and letting the boat drift a few yards on the current. Then he whipped the starting-cord on the small outboard motor. It caught at the second attempt and we moved downstream with the Daimler receding into the rain. We followed the bends gotten. But one memory persisted, the memory of the Austrian Jew as he talked about what he called 'the fently sveet but distinctive smell of veeping chelignite'. He'd passed down the aisles offering the open tin box for inspection. 'Schmell!' he promised, 'und you donn't forget!'

It was true and the unforgettable smell was rising from the bag between my legs. I put it down hastily then reminded myself that secondary explosives are safe enough unless detonated. Professor Rifkind's voice partially reassured me. 'Ebsolutely safe, chentlemen, ontless ignited by fuse-vire or bercussion ven it goes into detunnation almost imm*ed*iately!'

I froze, hearing the phone ring upstairs in the dead girl's apartment. The ringing persisted for fully five minutes before the caller hung up. It was getting on for two o'clock and I was hungry. I left the locked bag where it was and let myself out to the street. Twenty minutes later I was back at the houseboat. Gulls were quartering the river in the rain, their quarrelsome cries discordant. It was Friday and most of my neighbours had left for the country. The owner of the Herborium was the usual exception. His boat is a topheavy monstrosity painted red, blue and gold and which somehow manages to survive the winters. He closes his store at one o'clock on Saturday and spends the weekend brushing his dog and reading the life of Krishnamurti, The New Christ. The woman who cleans for me has another theory born of intense dislike for him. She claims that he spends his time sending radio-signals to Albania, a place located in her mind somewhere to the left of Singapore.

I unfastened my sitting-room door, savouring the

73

in the bank, the water becoming rougher. Salty spray
blew back in my face, stinging the bruised flesh above
my left ear. Burns knew his river or at least this part
of it, nosing the dinghy past corroded hulks and a
mobile garage selling fuel-oil to passing craft. A dog
bounded along the lighted deck, stiff-legged and snarling.
A man's shout was drowned on the wind. The Ratcatcher swung the tiller hard, bringing the boat round
in a wide half-circle. A forty-feet cruiser loomed out of
the murk. The name was painted in black on the grey
stern: *Skua-Ramsgate*.

Burns stopped the motor. The lighted wheelhouse
illuminated the small stern-deck of the cruiser. A man
in a shiny yellow stormcoat tossed a rope over the side.
The Ratcatcher caught it, holding the dinghy steady
and hauling in till he made fast, close to a boarding
ladder. He motioned me to go up. The man waiting
above gave me a hand, rolling easily with the movement
of the cruiser. The gun he was holding revived mem-
ories of firearms training. It was an Astra-Magnum .357,
the most powerful hand-weapon made. He spun me
with his free arm, propelling me towards the wheelhouse. It was warm and dry inside and I could smell
coffee brewing below. The man in the yellow slicker was
in his early thirties with a network of fine lines criss-
crossing the skin around his eyes and mouth. He was
well-built with swift sure movements and a look of cheer-
ful confidence. He hung his stormcoat on a hook and
turned, still pointing the gun at me.

'Take off that bleedin' cape,' he ordered, showing good
teeth. His hair was short and curly.

I slipped my head through the neck of the poncho
and took a look at my surroundings. The red leather

padding the spring-seat behind the wheel matched the upholstered benches. There was one of those revolving screens, a Decca Navigation System and lighted chart-table. The two fuel gauges showed both tanks to be full. Jerry and I had been aboard a similar boat the year before in Norway. They were fitted with two three-two-five Mercruiser motors, giving a range of two hundred miles at twenty-five knots. It was plain that no expense had been spared fitting out *Skua*. There was a ship-to-shore telephone, two-way radio and an open cupboard door revealed a range of exotic bottles. The Rat-catcher shut the wheelhouse door and opened another at the top of some rubber-treaded stairs. There was a glimpse of shaded lamps below, Dufy prints on the walls. He jerked his thumb and I went down the stairs.

The cabin below was carpeted in deep pile the colour of cobalt. The table was screwed to the floor, so were the two beds. Teresa Cintron was lying on one of them, her wrists and ankles tied behind her, her dark hair spread across the pillow. She was still wearing the outfit she had worn at the inquest, her tailored skirt hiked high. Olga's boyfriend was on the other bed, hands and feet tied in the same way, only his trousers and shoes had been removed. His face was haggard and afraid.

The Ratcatcher's voice sneered behind me. 'Paul Carpenter, meet Inspector Raven. You and the chick know one another already.'

Her eyes found mine imploringly but there was nothing I could do about it. They'd both been tied with nylon cord so that their arms and legs were pulled together in the small of their backs. I could see another cabin forrard while a short passage aft led to the galley and lavatory. Beyond these were the fuel-tanks and the motor-housings.

The Ratcatcher took off his coat and hat and sat at the table. 'See what the bastard has in his pockets, Jimbo.'

The curly-haired man was an expert at the job. Practised fingers searched all the right places, the hollow between my shoulderblades, my armpits and the insides of my thighs. He made me remove my shoes and belt and felt inside the neck of my sweater. He threw the contents of my pockets on the table.

'That's it. He's clean.'

The Ratcatcher poked at the pile in front of him, separating money, keys, cigarettes and lighter from the pouch containing Bertorelli's skeleton-keys. His eyes bulged.

'Where the fuck did these come from?'

'Somebody gave them to me,' I answered.

He offered his hideous smile. His hands were as repulsive as his face with square-nailed fingers and bent-back thumbs.

'Do ye no hear that, Jimbo! "Somebody gave them to me" he says – and him an ex-*po*-leess-man.'

Jimbo shook his head reprovingly. His heavy blue sweater bore the legend *Skua* across the chest.

'You'll have to watch it, mate. They'll do you for a nail-file these days.'

'Nah,' said the Ratcatcher. 'Not him. Old Bill takes care of his own. Isnae that right, Raven?'

I kept silent, trying to work out why Carpenter was a prisoner. The Ratcatcher's mood changed suddenly.

'Take off yer strides!' he ordered.

I looked at him dumbfounded. 'Take off my trousers?'

Jimbo nodded encouragement. 'Do as he says, mate. Don't be embarrassed. Your girlfriend's seen it all before.'

I stood in my shorts with my socks at half-mast. Jimbo rolled away along the passage like someone who is permanently involved in the first steps of some intricate dance. He came back from the galley, grinning cheerfully and waving a juice-squeezer at me. It was one of those gadgets with two cups set inside one another and held on a pivot, large enough to take half-an-orange. He placed it on the table in front of the Ratcatcher. The reflection of the riding-lights shone through a pane in the passage ceiling. The cabin was quiet except for the squeak of the mooring-ropes. The Ratcatcher leaned across the table, demonstrating the action of the juice-squeezer. The snubnosed revolver was at his elbow.

'Prop her up so she can see,' he said.

Jimbo stuffed another pillow under Teresa's head. I could see her face in the mirror. Tears were forcing their way past her closed eyelids.

'Listen to me, lassie,' said Burns. 'We're no squeamish here. Your friend's going to get his wee balls crushed if ye're no sensible.'

Jimbo slipped behind me quickly, kicking my legs apart and locking me in a half-nelson. The nerves crawled in my groin and I felt like throwing up. The Ratcatcher's voice was oddly prim.

'How long do ye know Raven?'

She shook her head from side to side, the tears still rolling down her cheeks. Burns was on his feet in a flash, almost running in his haste to stand over her.

'Ye'll talk, ye wee bitch or I'll ruin the pair of ye!'

She opened her eyes, her face desperate as she looked at me. 'He came to the school the night Olga died. I had never seen him before that in my life.'

The Ratcatcher glanced across at Carpenter and exchanged nods with Jimbo. Teresa's answer must have tallied with what Carpenter had said. The Ratcatcher stood in front of me, rapping me gently in the crotch with the juice-squeezer.

'You've been poking yer nose into other people's business, Raven.'

I'd been working on an answer ever since he laid me out but it had to come naturally. One false note and I was in even deeper trouble, assuming this to be possible.

'I've been doing the same as you have,' I said. 'Putting a deal together. No more, no less.'

Carpenter's face in the mirror was shocked and drawn but I had no sympathy for him. The Ratcatcher went into a crouch.

'You found the jelly in the basement at Clare Street. Why did ye leave it there?'

I was still locked in Jimbo's half-nelson. The pressure of his bicep was paining the lump above my ear.

'I tried to tell you earlier,' I said. 'But you didn't want to listen.'

'I didnae want to listen,' he repeated sarcastically.

'That's right,' I said doggedly. 'Give me my trousers and I'll explain.'

He brought his face close to mine as if his eyes could explore my brain.

'Aye,' he said stepping back. 'Aye, give him his trousers, Jimbo.'

Jimbo threw them at me, his voice regretful. 'It's a pity to cover up those gorgeous legs. My old mother ought to have been here. She's never seen the law with no clothes on.'

'Get the coffee,' said Burns. He held the thirty-eight on me as I climbed into my trousers.

Jimbo came back with two steaming mugs. The Rat-catcher sipped, made a face and spat. He put his mug down on the table.

'Am I going to be drinking *that* for the rest of the trip?'

Jimbo sniffed the coffee appreciatively. 'You'll drink a lot worse, mate. And there's something else while we're about it. We'll have to revise our schedule. It'll take me a good hour to make the Crouch in this weather. Another three to cross the Channel.'

There was something sinister about the way they discussed their plans in front of us, as if we were already dead. Burns sat down at the table, the shortbarrelled revolver lifting.

'Tell me, Raven.'

It was my only chance of survival and the only chance for the two on the beds behind me.

'It's a long story,' I said hesitantly.

'Ye'll make it a short one,' he snarled.

I braced myself. 'O.K. It all started with the girl who died, Olga Suchard. She worked for my sister.'

'We dinna give a shit aboot yer sister,' he said impatiently. 'Who told you the jelly was in that basement?'

I turned, indicating Teresa. She stared apprehensively but there was no way in which I could indicate that I was fighting for our lives.

'She did. We both gave evidence at the inquest. I was the one who found Olga's body. This one came up to me after we left the court. She said she wanted to talk to me. That's when she told me about the bag. I opened it.'

'Who told the law?' He wiped the spit from the cleft in his upper lip.

'Nobody told the law,' I insisted. 'She was too scared and I had my reasons.'

Something bumped against the side of the cruiser. The Ratcatcher swung his head questioningly.

'Driftwood.' Jimbo's grin was reassuring. 'The river-police went by half-an-hour ago. It'll be midnight before they're back.'

Burns pointed at Carpenter. 'What did she say about him?'

My palms and armpits were sweating. 'No more than that he was Olga's boyfriend. I don't think she *knew* any more. It was the fact that he'd left this bag with Olga that made me curious.'

His eyes bored in on me. 'The lassie gave ye the keys to the flat and ye opened the bag. What then?'

I shrugged. 'I was downstairs when Carpenter came to the house the first time. I followed you both to Tre-gunter Road. He went inside and you got out of the car. That's when the penny dropped.'

'What's that supposed to mean?' He sniffed suspici-ously.

'I recognised you.'

'Ye're a liar,' he shouted. 'I never laid eyes on ye before in my life!'

'You're being modest,' I said. 'Your mug shot was in the Police Gazette. There were flyers out on you. You haven't changed that much in seven-and-a-half years.'

'It's the nick,' Jimbo cut in. 'Pure water, no women

and regular hours.' His airy manner faded under the Ratcatcher's scowl.

'Then what?' demanded Burns. I had the feeling that he was less sure of himself than he appeared to be.

'I followed the pair of you back to Clare Street. You collected the bag and I lost you outside Harrods.'

He mulled over the statement as if probing for inconsistencies. Jimbo was leaning against the stairs. The Ratcatcher lifted his head like a snake about to strike.

'And ye've no said a word to Old Bill aboot any of this?'

'Not one word,' I said resolutely. 'Is that so strange? I'm no different to anyone else. When there's a chance to score, I take it.'

'Aye,' he mused. 'You asked the Bishop where I lived. And ye were there tonight.'

'I was there,' I admitted. 'The more I knew about what was going on the better chance I had to make a deal.'

He rose from the table and came towards me, his hands on his hips. 'Then ye *were* on the take,' he said softly.

I shrugged. 'No more than the others. Everyone was at it. Everyone who had the chance.'

'Don't go for it,' Jimbo said suddenly. 'The monkey's lying.'

I ignored him, concentrating on Burns. 'I may not be a cop any longer but I still have the right connections.'

'Aye,' he drawled. 'Ye would have.'

'Can I have a cigarette?' I asked. The further I went the less plausible it sounded but there was no going back. He passed me a smoke and my lighter. 'You've been away a long time,' I continued. 'Things have changed since your day. The old Ghost Squad's gone.

Something called C11 has taken its place.'

The Ratcatcher looked across at Jimbo. 'You ever hear of C11?'

Jimbo nodded. 'They're here, there and everywhere – floaters. Crawling under people's beds and listening to what you dream about. You know, mystery men.'

The Ratcatcher's pale eyes narrowed. 'And what have they got to do with me?'

'Well,' I said. 'For one thing they've got a list of what they call target-criminals. Once you're on that list any-thing goes. They break rules the same way you people do. There's no nonsense about search-warrants and the like. These people turn your place over and you never know that they've been there.'

He cracked one knuckle after another, slowly. 'And ye're telling me that I'm on this list, is that it?'

I shook my head. 'No you're not. The point is that I could get you on.'

His face seamed and he broke into open laughter. 'Could ye no get Jimbo on as well?'

I managed to keep my voice steady. 'I'm serious, Burns. Once you're on that list you're C11's property. Nobody else has the right to touch you. And I'll know each time that an inquiry is made about you, whenever someone asks for your file. More than that, I'll know what C11 intends to do with their information.'

He was silent, his pale eyes flicking over my face. 'It can only happen once,' I urged. 'But once should be enough for a man like you. This is a foolproof guaran-tee—a licence to steal. All you have to do is choose the right caper.'

He thought for a minute. 'And just what do you get out of it?'

It had to be high to sound right. 'Fifty per cent. There are other people involved.'

Jimbo's derisive grin seemed to act as a trigger. The Ratcatcher's face set in pure hatred.

'What do ye think I am, ye wee blethering bastard! Detective Inspector, was it! Ye're just one of those piss-elegant buggers who eats peas on the back of a fork. I wouldn't touch the like of ye with a bargepole. Putting good people inside and you the biggest villain of the lot. Ye're nothing but a fucking con-man!'

My hands flew to my head as he grabbed me by the hair. 'A foolproof guarantee!' he screeched. '*You're* the best guarantee I ever had. Tie the bugger up, Jimbo, and make sure of the knots!'

Jimbo fished a length of cord from his pocket, smiling his choirboy smile.

'Fasten your seatbelt, mate.'

He shoved me down, leaning on me till my nose was touching the carpet. 'Hands behind your back, wrists together,' he instructed.

He knelt on me, wrenching the knots tightly together. He shifted his weight and dragged on the cord. The pressure forced my feet up, causing my back to arch. He turned me on my side and patted my cheek.

'All you need now is a lemon in your mouth. You're perfect.'

The Ratcatcher pulled a drawer in the table and swept the contents of my pockets into it. 'Where's their stuff?' he said, jerking his head at the pair on the beds.

'In the other drawer,' said Jimbo. He produced a couple of stopwatches, set them and gave one to Burns.

The Ratcatcher wiped his eyes and mouth. He was

sweating profusely. 'How soon after three can ye be there?'

Jimbo strapped his watch on. 'Three-thirty. On the dot.'

'There's nae chance of ye missing the creek?'

Jimbo blew hard. 'We've gone over all this at least twenty times,' he said wearily. 'Look, I know the Crouch like the back of my bleeding hand. I can navigate it upside down. I'll be tied up by the jetty waiting for you. There's nothing nearer than Seldon and you've seen that for yourself. A couple of farmers who go to bed at the same time as their cows.'

The Ratcatcher shrugged into his overcoat. 'And ye're sure aboot the customs?'

Jimbo was humouring him. 'I'm sure about the customs. I've done the run four times without seeing so much as a uniform. The only danger could come from a helicopter at Sheerness. And at three o'clock in the morning in this weather you can forget it.'

The Ratcatcher's furtive eyes slid from the two beds to linger on me.

'Take good care of these three, now. Remember they're part of the contract.'

'Don't you worry about a thing,' said Jimbo and closed one eye expressively.

He led the way up the stairs to the wheelhouse. His fingers found the light-switch and the cabin went dark except for the reflection of the riding lights coming through the passage window. I heard the two men crossing the deck, the rope slap against the side of the cruiser. Then the dinghy stuttered shorewards.

CHAPTER NINE

The wheelhouse doors were closed now but I could hear Jimbo moving around. He tuned the radio in to a Dutch station belting out Judy Garland. There was a sliver of light at the head of the stairs. With this and the reflection from the passage my eyes gradually refocused. The beds took on shape. Teresa was still lying on her stomach. Her head was placed so that she seemed to be looking at me.

'It was lies,' I whispered hoarsely. 'I was trying to bluff our way out.' She didn't answer.

I was lying on the floor, trussed like a chicken, about three feet away from her bed. She moved her head, reluctantly, disapprovingly, I couldn't tell. All I could see was the darkness of her hair against the pillow. It suddenly mattered to me that she understood.

I kept my voice very low. 'Did you hear me, Teresa. Everything I said just now was a lie.'

I could just hear her answer. 'I know.'

A muffled roar came from the far end of the passage and the hull began to vibrate. Propellers churned and the cruiser gathered way, heading downstream. The noise of the motors made it possible to speak without whispering. I was near enough to smell the scent released by the warmth of her body.

'I want you to tell me what happened—how you got here.'

She shook her head, dislodging a strand of hair from her eyes so that she could see me. Her voice was accusing.

'It was Paul. He came to my house this afternoon. He said that Olga's father had asked me to go to the flat and pack her clothes for him. I believed him. It all sounded so true. And then . . .' Her voice wavered.

'Tell me,' I urged. 'It's important.'

It took a few seconds but she pulled herself together. 'I could see we were going the wrong way. I knew that Olga's father was in an hotel on Piccadilly. He said so in court. But Paul kept saying that everything was all right, that I shouldn't worry. Finally we went to some house and that terrible man was waiting there with a negro.'

She went quiet again. The boat had moved closer to the shore. Fingers of light were reaching across the cabin ceiling. The galley-door had unhooked itself and was banging. I could hear the music still playing up in the wheelhouse.

'You've got to tell me what happened,' I begged.

'They put me in this room,' she said in a low voice. 'I could hear them all downstairs talking, quarrelling. Paul and that man. Then we came here in a car. I am sorry but I am very frightened.' She said it like a small lost girl.

I looked across at the other bed. 'You must be proud of yourself.'

There was no reply. 'Carpenter,' I said.

'Yes.'

'You'd better start talking,' I said.

He lifted his head off the pillow. 'What are you? Some sort of knight in shining armour?' His tone was almost

127

hostile. There was no hint of regret, no concern apparently even for his own life.

I tried to reason with him. 'Listen to me, Carpenter. Don't you realise why that pair of thugs didn't worry about talking in front of us? *I'll* tell you why. It's because as far as they're concerned we're as good as dead. They're going to put us over the side somewhere in the middle of the Channel and it'll be months before our bodies are found. If ever.'

The door opened at the head of the stairs and the lights came on. Jimbo peered down from the wheelhouse. His yellow slicker was wet as if he'd been out on deck. It must have been the banging of the galley door that bothered him. He located the source of the noise, came down and fastened the door and went up again. I looked up at the cabin windows. All I could see from where I lay was spray. I kept my voice low, looking across at Carpenter.

'Can you see where we are?'

He raised his head. 'Nothing. It's pitch-dark out there.'

The two powerful motors had been throttled back and the cruiser was barely under way. The strident blast of a foghorn reverberated through the cabin, leaving my ears ringing. I braced myself for some sort of collision, picturing the wreckage of the boat, helping hands pulling us out of the water. A couple of minutes went by and the blast sounded again. The noise sounded as if it was coming from the top of the wheelhouse. I realised that it was a mechanical foghorn. Safety regulations required its use in bad visibility and Jimbo was taking no chances.

'Listen to me, Carpenter,' I said. 'There's still a chance for us but I have to know what's going on.'

128

I sensed rather than saw the movement of his head. 'What can you do?' he demanded. 'What can anyone do?'

His self-pity was even worse than his hostility. 'The police are out looking for us at this very moment,' I urged. 'We've got to make contact with them somehow. But I have to know the truth. It's too late for lies.'

The last few minutes seemed to have cut him down to size and he lay still and quiet. Teresa's voice was cold and contemptuous.

'You waste your time. This man is a coward.'

The words stung him to answer. 'I don't care what you people think. What the hell can you know? I loved Olga. Everything I did was for her.'

I'd heard it all before in similar circumstances. They always do it for someone else, as though this achieves some miraculous shift in moral values. My guess was that there wasn't a generous thought in the whole of Carpenter's body. The only person he really cared about was himself. I waited till the echo of the foghorn died away.

'You planned a robbery with Burns. *Where?*'

His voice was shaky. 'I didn't know till I picked up the newspaper on the plane this morning and read that she was dead. Do you think I'd have *left* her if I'd known that she was pregnant!'

'Her death couldn't have bothered you that much,' I said pointedly. 'You were in that house searching the place for the bag.'

'Because I *had* to,' he said desperately. 'Look. I wanted to give Olga all the things she deserved. Once I realised that she was dead there was no point in going on. It was Burns who wouldn't let me back out. He threatened to tell the bank. What's it all about, Raven? Why did she have to die?'

There was no time for emotional luxuries and I was deliberately brutal.

'She died because she didn't want your child.'

We looked at one another across the darkened cabin. 'You're a real bastard, aren't you?' he said bitterly. 'But it's not true. Olga loved me.'

'Then prove yourself worthy of it. You can save three people's lives including your own.'

He gave a sort of strangled sigh. 'What does it matter? What does anything matter? O.K. What do you want to know?'

'The name of the bank to start with.'

'The Union Bank of Kuwait. It's in Stanhope Gate, at the bottom of Park Lane. I've been working there for four years. The manager flies to Kuwait once a month and I'm left in charge of the keys from Friday to Monday.'

It was all falling into place. 'That's the keys to the vault?'

His head moved restlessly. 'No, the manager keeps those. He leaves me with the keys to the front doors and the key that operates the security system. You see, we're a small bank but we always carry a reserve of at least half-a-million pounds. In cash. Arab visitors think nothing of sending out for sums like thirty or forty thousand. If it's not there when they want it, they simply take their accounts away.'

It hung together so far. London was full of stories popularly accepted as true. About Sheikhs carrying dispatch-cases stuffed with banknotes, call girls rewarded with Cadillacs.

'We wanted to go to Brazil,' he said remotely. 'We could have been happy there together.'

Teresa's voice spat from her bed. 'A thief and a liar. My *God*, how I despise you!'

'What about you?' he retorted. 'Olga would still be alive if it hadn't been for you!'

'Shut up, the pair of you!' I rolled over, fighting the first agony of cramp. 'Who's got the keys now?'

'El Hami,' he said. He was listening and paying attention. 'The manager. Burns had copies made before I gave them back the last time.'

It was the first false note. If Burns had the keys then he didn't need Carpenter. I said so.

'He needed me, all right,' affirmed Carpenter. 'There's a combination lock as well as a key on the switch that works the security system. The combination's changed every Monday. I knew it the day before I went to Zürich. I gave it to Burns this morning.'

The cramp in my thigh was easing. I lay perfectly still, not daring to move till the muscle had completely relaxed.

'You're a fool,' I said.

'I know it.'

'Exactly when is Burns supposed to hit this bank—do you know that or not?'

'Tonight sometime. He'd never say exactly when. I was supposed to meet him at seven o'clock in the morning and get my share of the money. Then he was taking Olga and me in the boat to Belgium. That's why I went to Zürich. To open a bank account.'

Rain buffeted the windows. The cruiser was barely crawling. We were talking in snatches, hurrying the words between blasts of the foghorn. 'Where did you meet Burns?'

'Through a man I was at school with, a journalist. I told him I was writing a book about bank robbery and needed background material. He found Burns and arranged a meeting. From then on it seemed to go like clockwork. Whatever he wanted I supplied him with. Have you seen the Daimler?'

'I've had the benefit of a ride in it,' I said grimly.

'It's going up,' he said. I could see his pale hair hanging as he raised his head again. 'Trinny's leaving it in Curzon Street with a charge of explosive in the boot. That's no more than a few hundred yards from the bank. It's going up at the same time Burns blows the vaults.'

He was no match for a pro like the Ratcatcher. The synchronised explosions were a sophisticated touch that would send everyone running in the wrong direction. A car blown up on the street would be taken as evidence of yet another I.R.A. outrage. Police, fire-brigades, ambulances and bomb-disposal units would zero in on the wrong target while a few yards away the Ratcatcher stepped from the bank with a fortune.

I rolled towards Teresa's bed. No matter how carefully I moved I seemed to land on a piece of bruised flesh.

'How much courage do you have, Teresa?'

'I do not want to die,' she answered steadily.

'This guy upstairs is as much a killer as Burns. You realise that?'

This time she didn't answer. 'He'll smell a rat,' I said, 'if one of us asks to use the lavatory but there's a chance that he'll listen to you. I'll try to get his attention as you go past the galley. See if you can grab something.'

'A knife?'

Her voice was resolute. I had a quick picture of the knife against Jimbo's throat, the blood spurting as he moved his head.

'Do you think you can do it?'

'If I must then I can,' she replied.

I wriggled my way back to the wall. 'Yell,' I instructed. 'And make it loud!'

It was a while before the wheelhouse door opened. Salt air freshened the stuffy cabin. Jimbo stared down from the patch of light, swaying with the movement of the boat.

'What's all the hollering and hooting?' he demanded suspiciously.

'I have to go to the lavatory,' Teresa called back.

We were entering deeper water and the cabin-cruiser was unsteady. We needed more speed to lift the bows and give the boat stability. Jimbo reached behind and opened the throttle a couple of notches. He held the wheel steady with one hand as our rhythm increased.

'You have to do *what*?' he demanded.

She told him and added, 'Please!' He turned his head, his face tinged green from the light of the facia-board. He was looking out through the revolving windshield.

'She's a woman, for God's sake,' I croaked from the floor.

'Belt up!' he snapped. He headed *Skua* into the wind and threw the motors out of gear. Our forward movement ceased and the cruiser started to wallow. The cabin lights came on. Jimbo made the stairs down in two leaps, the heavy gun in his left hand. His sleeves were rolled up showing muscled forearms blotched with freckles. Teresa lay quite still as he untied her. Then she swung her feet to the floor, pulling down her skirt and rubbing her chafed wrists. He nodded in the direction of the passage.

'You've got exactly three minutes.'

Her eyes and nose were red but she spoke with dignity. 'Thank you.'

He followed her into the passage and leaned against the galley-door. 'Starting as of now,' he said, looking at the stopwatch on his wrist.

The lavatory-door closed behind her. He grinned as though he had read my thoughts. All I could hope for was a miracle. A window large enough for Teresa to crawl through and her courage to swim for the shore.

Jimbo was still grinning at me. 'I don't know who you are,' I said. 'But I can't believe you're a cold-blooded murderer.'

He glanced sideways through the heavy glass windows, interpreting the sounds of the river.

'You never know *what* you'll do, mate. Not even you and you're an educated man.'

He whistled cheerfully and winked again. A thought seemed to occur and he demonstrated how the window worked. It opened no more than a couple of inches then was held by a brake on the hinge.

'They're all like that,' he volunteered. 'She'd need to be a midget.'

He leaned back against the galley-door, the motors quietly grumbling, the boat almost stationary.

'You must know what he's going to do,' I challenged. 'He's going to kill us, isn't he?'

His grin held but his eyes were oddly furtive. 'You've been watching too much television.'

I did my best to put a hole in his confidence. 'You'll be the only witness. You think he's going to walk off this boat and leave you alive?'

'Don't you worry about me, mate,' he said easily. 'I can take care of myself.'

Something in his face gave me the clue. I understood that no matter what the Ratcatcher had in mind, Jimbo had his own ideas about the loot.

'He'll run rings round you,' I promised. But the heart had gone out of my voice. It came to me that whatever the outcome between Burns and Jimbo, I wouldn't be there to see it.

He banged on the lavatory-door. 'Time's up!'

I couldn't hear what Teresa answered but it was clearly the wrong thing. Jimbo braced himself, lifted a knee and let his foot fly against the door, the whole of his weight behind it. The impact tore the lock from the screws.

'Get back in the cabin!' he growled.

She came out, holding her head high. He chided her as he retied her bonds, his tone a mixture of annoyance and confidence. He wiped his forehead with the back of a freckled hand.

'All right, you scurvy fuckers, now listen to me! You've had your fun and it's over. The next time I come down here it'll be for one reason and one reason only. You'd better remember it.'

He went up the stairs, flicked off the cabin-lights and slammed the door to the wheelhouse. Seconds later the motors increased their speed. Teresa's whisper was hoarse in the sudden darkness.

'I'm sorry.'

I disregarded the words, the memory of our failure.

Adrenalin was driving new hope through my veins. An image had formed in my mind, recreating something seen or heard. I wormed to the side of Teresa's bed, knowing instinctively that she was a better bet than Carpenter for what I needed.

'Roll off,' I ordered. 'Just relax and let yourself go. You'll land on top of me.'

I turned on my stomach. The bed creaked and she let herself go, her body falling across mine. She gasped as I shouldered her off.

'Turn on your side and come close,' I said.

She turned obediently. We were lying back to back with our bound hands touching. Both of us were tied in precisely the same way, a length of nylon cord connecting the two clove-hitches around our wrists and ankles. The knotted end of the rope was somewhere in the small of my back.

'Your fingers are better than mine,' I urged. 'See if you can find the end of the rope.'

She struggled and stopped despairingly. 'My nails are breaking.'

'Let 'em break,' I said. Her body was close against mine in a strange warm intimacy, her hair tickling the back of my neck.

'You're up too high,' she complained. I wriggled down till she stopped me. '*Now!* Stay like that!'

Rain was still pelting against the windows but something was missing from the sound-pattern. I realised that the foghorn was silent. Carpenter spoke shakily.

'We're passing some sort of town. I can see the lights.'

The visibility must have improved. I reckoned that I'd been on board for about an hour-and-a-half, say ten miles or so. Since Carpenter was facing the north bank, that would put us somewhere near Tilbury.

'It's undone!' Teresa's whisper was exultant. 'I've undone it!'

I strained all my muscles, stretching my body till ankles and wrists drew away from one another. The rope was still round my hands. I pushed them against her fingers. Suddenly I was free, the nylon cord loose on the carpet. I stuffed it in my pocket and untied Teresa. She held me close, still kneeling, pressing her wet cheek against mine. I remembered the man in Venezuela and the memory left me vaguely resentful. I took her face between my palms.

'It's going to be all right now. Just do what I tell you and it'll be all right.'

I untied Carpenter and gave him his shoes and trousers. He sat on the bed, trying to get the circulation back to his legs and arms. We were three against one but Jimbo was hardly overmatched.

I looked down at Carpenter. 'Have you made up your mind whose side you're on?'

He hunched a shoulder. 'What the hell does it matter. The moment he catches on that we're free he's coming down here shooting. You heard what he said. We'll be sitting targets.'

I brought my face close to his. 'You're beginning to get on my nerves. I asked you a question.'

'I don't have a choice,' he said.

The realities of fear are strange. It's difficult to hate a man with whom you're sharing a common danger but I was close to it.

'You've got a choice,' I answered. 'A few years in jail or be dead.'

He took a deep breath. 'Take me with you.'

The cruiser was cutting through the water smoothly, the bows high under the thrust of the twin-screws. It was the lavatory-door that was banging now, just hanging from its screws. Teresa came after me as I ran along the passage, her fingers clinging to my sweater. The headroom decreased. Fuel and fresh water tanks were fitted into the forepart, the two Mercruiser motors installed on each side of the passage. Inspection lights showed the chromed compact engines sweetly humming. There were no tools. Everything seemed to be up in the wheelhouse. I shut the panel-doors. Teresa watched my face anxiously, trying to read my mind.

I led her forrard to the master cabin. Carpenter came after us. I dared not put the lights on but I could make out the wide bed and fitted cupboards. There was an airline overnight bag on the bed. I took it to the window. Inside was a black leather jacket neatly folded on top of corduroy trousers. Both were new. I felt in the side compartment, coming up with a driving licence in the name of Dougal Harris. Deeper down was a British passport issued in the same name. It was franked with a Brazilian visa good for the next six months. The holder's occupation was given as 'manufacturer's agent'. The Ratcatcher's face stared at me from the title page, harelip covered with a moustache and wearing spectacles over his baleful little eyes. I stuffed the passport in my pocket and threw the bag back on the bed.

I searched till I found what I was looking for, a brass seacock in the shower stall, positioned a couple of inches above the duckboards. There was a squareheaded wrench attached to it. The cock was the same type as the one in the other cabin, a tube through the double hull, beneath the surface of the water with a valve to prevent accidental flooding. I stumbled as the cruiser pitched violently. The wind had got up and we were hitting the wave-crests hard. For the moment at least Jimbo had his hands full. Gusts pounded the windows, spray streaming off as the bows lifted again. The glass cleared briefly. I saw the blue lamp of a police-launch in the distance. It vanished in the same second. We moved back to the other cabin. I opened the table drawers, retrieving the things that had been taken from us. There was a snapshot of Olga among Carpenter's possessions. Teresa's first move was an incredible use of her hand-mirror. She tidied her hair, put the mirror back in her bag and smiled at me. I pointed at the brass disc in the hull beneath the windows.

'I'm going to open both those sea-cocks. That and the one in the other cabin.'

Carpenter pushed his hand through his yellow hair, his face nervous. 'You'll sink the boat, for God's sake.'

'Try praying,' I retorted. 'You must be good at something.'

I estimated that we were travelling at half-speed now, Jimbo driving the cruiser on the hump, keeping the bows well ahead of the wind-propelled water.

'Let's go,' I said. 'I want you two up on the bed.'

They followed me into the master-cabin and climbed up, Teresa tucking her legs under her and looking at me with confidence. She was twice the man that Carpenter was. The cock in the showerstall was stiff with disuse. I put a foot on the end of the wrench and leaned my weight on it. The valve gradually opened. The dribble of water became a jet. I kicked the wrench down as far as it would go. The river spurted in under pressure, gushing into the middle of the showerstall.

I pulled the plastic curtains wide and stepped back into the cabin. 'When he opens that door he may be shooting. Keep well out of sight.'

Water had already flooded the bottom of the shower-stall and was spreading across the carpeted floor. I ran through to the other cabin, taking the wrench with me, and wedged a chair behind the stairs leading up to the wheelhouse. The next thing to do was take the lamps out of their sockets. The second sea-cock was even harder to unfasten but the banging of the wrench was lost in the sound of the motors. A cold, formidable jet smelling of the very bottom of the river shot across the floor, missing me by inches. I kept the wrench in my hand and clambered up on the chair behind the stairs. The water was already a foot deep and pouring in from both ends of the boat, sloshing against the hull. The level was climbing steadily. I was gambling that the shifting weight would affect the steering. Jimbo would probably check the rudder and couplings before investigating below. There was no way now of closing the sea-cocks and escape could only be through the door overhead. The cruiser veered sharply, first in one direction then in the other. The boat turned again, this time in an arc. Suddenly it stopped, wallowing on the ebbing tide. Jimbo had either switched off the motors or water had got to them.

CHAPTER TEN

The door opened above my head. I saw Jimbo's arm stretch out, feeling for the light-switch. It clicked uselessly. He grabbed a flashlight from the locker, the gun in his other hand showing in the beam of light. I heard him suck his breath in as he saw what lay below.

'Jesus *Christ*!' he burst out.

He came down a couple of steps, going forwards this time instead of backwards. I shoved my hands through the stair-treads from behind, grabbed his ankles and yanked hard, bracing my knees against the stairs. He pitched forward, his weight wrenching his feet from my grasp. His flashlight spiralled into the air then the stairs shook as his head hit the upright. I lowered myself into waist-high water, shouting for the others to come. They waded out from the master-cabin holding their hands high above their heads. Jimbo was floating on his back, his head bumping against the hull. Flashlight and gun were somewhere under the water which was still pouring into the boat. The light from the wheelhouse shone down on the oily surface.

I pushed Jimbo's body towards the stairs. 'Help me get him up,' I gasped.

He was limp and heavy and it took the three of us to wrestle him up to the wheelhouse. I laid him out on the floor and we stood there looking at one another. We were soaked from the waist down, miserable-looking and worst of all afraid. Suddenly all the lights went out, the green glow on the facia-board fading gradually. Even the navigation-lights on the mast overhead were extinguished. We were half-a-mile from the shore and drifting out to sea on the ebbing tide. My lighter was still working. I held the flame close to Jimbo's face. His eyes were shut but I was taking no chances. I pulled the length of cord from my pocket, turned Jimbo over and put a hitch around his wrists. The word MAYDAY was stencilled on the top of one of the lockers. Inside was a selection of orange-coloured life jackets, a Very pistol and flares.

Teresa's voice was very quiet and close to me. 'I think that we are sinking, John.' I'd no idea how or when she had learned my first name but she used it perfectly naturally. Maybe if I'd been less selfish or even younger . . .

I looked out through the window. It was difficult to see anything but I could feel that we were drifting, hear the water breaking over the stern. I gave them each a life-preserver and put Jimbo's on like a strait-jacket, fastening his arms inside. He was conscious now and managed a wry grin.

'You crafty fucker, I should have known.'

I propped him up on a locker. 'We're going down by the helm. Do you want to stay aboard?'

He treasured the ghost of his grin, his eyes willing my destruction. I looked from Teresa to Carpenter.

'Can you both swim?'

Carpenter nodded. 'I'm good for a mile.' He was the young hero ready for action. I think that at that moment he'd forgotten how he came to be there.

Teresa was more doubtful. 'I can float.'

I loaded the Very pistol, stepped out on deck and fired. The flare soared up into the rain, its flashing tail an appeal for help but there was no one to answer our call. Visibility was fair. There were no other boats in sight. Lights twinkled across the dark expanse of water on the south bank of the river. It was difficult to gauge how far away they were but I put it at four or five hundred yards. The stern of the boat was completely awash, the craft barely moving under the weight of the water she had shipped. The end could only be minutes away.

There were plastic bags in one of the other lockers. I wrapped the flares and pistol separately, put the contents of my pockets into a third bag and stuffed them all inside my sweater. My poncho was somewhere below. The roll of nylon cord Jimbo had used on us was at the bottom of the same storage-locker. I fastened one end to Carpenter's waist. He looked down, his face tense as I tied the knot. I measured off three yards, looped the rope round Teresa, measured a second length and attached it to my belt. The rope linked us together but left each with freedom of movement.

Jimbo's wet hair had sprung into tight golden curls. His face was resigned, a lump growing in the centre of his forehead.

'We're all going over the side together,' I told him. 'Make one wrong move and you're on your own.'

I gave the others plastic bags. 'Put your stuff somewhere safe and get ready to jump. You go first,' I said to Carpenter.

We lined up on the starboard side of the sinking boat, the wind blowing the rain in our faces.

'*Now!*' I shouted and the four of us jumped, hitting

the water together. My fingers were locked in the collar of Jimbo's lifejacket. We struggled in the cold choppy river, the rope tugging at my waist. We were swimming one behind the other, Carpenter leading. His arms and legs thrashed in an unco-ordinated crawl, kicking the water back in Teresa's face. I could hear her gasping for breath as she floundered. I trod water desperately, yanking on the rope and shouting at the bodies bobbing in front of me.

'It's no good like this! Stick to the breaststroke and kick together!'

I could see Carpenter pointing and turned my head. The cabin-cruiser was fifty yards away, half-submerged, her bows at an angle of ninety degrees to the water. She vanished suddenly, without noise or drama.

We took our time from there, our legs working in unison and our progress was steady, helped by the wind and the tide. The cluster of lights on the shore grew brighter. I could see a jetty, support-piles sticking up out of the mud, stone steps cut in the embankment. Carpenter was the first to find bottom. He stood erect, hauling us in on the rope. Jimbo came up off his knees and we all waded forward, out of the sucking mud on to a hoop of dirty sand and shingle littered with plastic containers. I unfastened my lifejacket at the foot of the steps. Teresa, Carpenter and I stepped free of the rope. An inn-sign was creaking under the light at the top of the stone steps. Teresa wrung the water from her hair, head bent sideways as she smiled at me. I groped inside my sweater and pulled the plastic bags out. I stuck a flare in the Very pistol and showed it to Jimbo.

'I don't know what this thing'll do to your brains but we can always find out.'

His composure was back in spite of his plight. His face assumed a pained expression.

'Why don't you give over! I'm catching my death of cold and you're threatening me with violence.'

He had a certain style, I suppose. I represented the difference between a fortune and years of imprisonment but he could still manage Cockney irony. I remembered the Ratcatcher with a sense of urgency. Everything was suddenly possible again. I'd forgotten to take off my watch and it had stopped. I shoved Jimbo towards the steps, following close behind him. He was out-of-breath and blowing at the top. There was an open space in front of the brickbuilt inn. A narrow hedgebound lane overhung with telephone wires disappeared into the darkness. The rain had miraculously stopped and we were within reach of civilisation. Trees dripped in the unheralded silence. There was nothing there but the inn. The doors were closed but the lights in the bar were on. I pushed Jimbo close to one of the bow-windows and peeped into the taproom. Brassbound beer-engines glistened in the light of a dying coal-fire. There were Toby jugs hanging on hooks behind the bar and prints of shire-horses on the walls. I rapped on the glass with the pistol-butt. The woman standing in front of the fire turned sharply, her fingers flying to her throat. She was middle-aged with smooth grey hair, a lavender wool dress and a string of wooden beads around her neck, what Cathy would have called a *'comfortable* woman'. I tapped again and she came towards the window, peering uncertainly.

'There's been an accident,' I yelled. 'We need some help.'

I don't suppose she could hear but what she saw sent

her back behind the bar and through a door out of my sight. A couple of minutes later, bolts rattled and the taproom door was thrown wide. Framed in the entrance was a humpty-dumpty in blue flannel shirtsleeves and corduroy carpet slippers. His round head appeared to be attached to his rolypoly body without aid of a neck and his dark eyes glistened like goats' droppings. He was holding a doublebarrelled shotgun in a way that suggested he knew how to use it. A Doberman bitch held on a leash by the woman snarled at us, head low and white fangs exposed.

'It's after hours,' the man said in a no-nonsense country burr. 'And we don't do rooms nor food.'

He sounded like someone dealing with an obstreperous bus-party. 'Our boat sank,' I said lamely. 'We had to swim for it.'

His gaze settled on Jimbo who winked back, his arms still imprisoned inside the lifejacket.

'*He* swam for it?' the landlord demanded incredulously.

'I towed him,' I said.

'Towed him,' he repeated. The information didn't appear to help.

'Look,' I said. 'It's difficult to explain but can I use your phone? I have to contact the police.'

'Shut the door on them, Ed,' the woman said quickly. Her motherly face was apprehensive. 'I don't trust them.' The Doberman growled softly in sympathy.

'I know what I'm doing,' he said stoutly. 'What's going on?' he demanded looking at Teresa now. 'What do you want the police for?'

I'd come too far to be thwarted by some rustic inn-keeper. I leaned forward, blinking in the light,

146

letting him take a good look at my face.

'A serious crime is about to be committed and it's your duty to assist me in preventing it. Refuse and you'll find yourself in a whole lot of trouble.'

'All right,' he said guardedly. 'But you don't come in here without giving me that there pistol.'

I handed the Very pistol to him, butt first. He shut the door behind us and spoke quietly to the woman. She let the bitch off the chain-leash. The Doberman sniffed at us each in turn then sank on the floor in front of the door, her front legs crossed.

'She won't harm you,' the landlord said easily. 'No more'n a baby would. Just don't come too near the wife or myself.'

Teresa's face was very white and she was shivering. I kicked life into the fire and wrapped an arm round Teresa's shaking shoulders.

'Have you got something dry to lend her?' I spoke to the landlord's wife. 'A blanket would help.'

It took her no more than seconds to decide. Her smile made her ten years younger.

She fussed forward, taking Teresa by the arm. 'You come along with me, my dear. We'll soon get you warmed up good and proper.'

Teresa looked at me for guidance. It was a good feeling for me and I saw her go reluctantly.

'I'll be here,' I promised.

The two women vanished through the door behind the bar. I heard their footsteps as they climbed the stairs. Carpenter and Jimbo were sitting on a bench in front of the fire, their clothes beginning to steam. The Doberman watched with wary almond eyes as the landlord shuffled behind the bar and placed his shotgun on the counter. The phone was on a shelf under the mirror. He dialled with his back to us.

'George? It's Ed. That's right, Ed Spinney.' He coughed and turned the cough into an embarrassed laugh. 'Look, George. I got a rum lot here in the pub, three men and a girl saying as their boat's gone down. *Sunk*. No I have *not* been drinking.' He held the receiver away from his ear, looking indignantly at his reflection in the mirror. 'Anyway you get over here right away,' he continued. 'And bring someone with you.'

He hung up, swung round and propped his pear-shaped belly against the edge of the counter.

'Our sergeant's on his way. He'll sort you out. You can have a drink if you like but you can't pay for it. We don't want no lawbreaking.'

'That's more like it,' Jimbo said promptly. 'Make mine a large rum and stick a straw in the glass so I can drink it.'

The landlord glanced at him curiously. 'What you got him tied up like that for?'

I crossed the room and went behind the bar. 'Don't waste your sympathy. He may be a clown but he's also a killer. That thing doesn't come off till the police get here.'

The landlord produced the drink. I held the glass of rum-and-water to Jimbo's mouth. He drank it down in two gulps and belched. I mistrusted the jovial resignation profoundly. I asked the landlord if I could use the phone. The emergency-operator accepted the code-call and transferred me to the Metropolitan Mobile switchboard. It was some time before they managed to raise Mallory. He came on the line, terse and uncompromising.

'What the fuck is this? Where've you been? I've got two cars running about all over London looking for you!'

'If Jerry's with you let me talk to him,' I said.

I heard the noise of traffic in the background then Jerry Soo's voice.

'John?'

'There's no time for questions,' I told him. 'All you do is listen. The name of the bank, the Ratcatcher's routine, everything. And I've got something else, a couple of candidates for the slammer. Olga's boyfriend and a chum. Tell Mallory I'm going to leave them with the local law. Hold it a minute.'

I glanced back at the landlord. 'What's the name of this place – the nearest town?'

'Bolton. If you want the police district it comes under Rochester.'

I passed the news on to Jerry. 'Tell Mallory he can make his own arrangements about having this pair picked up. The girl's clean and she's with me.'

'Understood,' he said quickly. And then on a note of curiosity. 'What's the matter with your voice?'

'It's been in the river,' I said. A picture had formed with disturbing clarity, a picture of a car packed with gelignite left to explode in the heart of Mayfair. I don't know what it was exactly, a doubt that Mallory might not keep his word, perhaps. But the closer we came to the crunch the less I felt like sharing all my information. But I was close when the I.R.A. bombed the Hilton. I've *seen* people running blindly in shock, stumps of arms spurting blood – maimed children crawling and crying for help. I couldn't gamble with the lives of innocent folk.

'Listen, Jerry,' I said. 'There's a Daimler parked some-where along Curzon Street. Probably at the Park Lane end.' I gave the number of the car. 'The boot's stuffed with gelignite. It's going to hit the roof at the same time as the Ratcatcher performs so that everyone's running in the wrong direction. Tell Mallory to approach with extreme caution.'

Jerry spoke in a rapid aside. He was back with a new brusqueness in his tone.

'He wants to know when and where, John.'

I could see the faces of the others in the bar-mirror. Carpenter's eyes were closed, Jimbo was grinning, the landlord's mouth was slack.

'John?' Jerry's voice was thin in the phone. 'This could mean calling in the Bomb Squad. You realise that?'

They were promoting unnecessary problems. 'The bank's nothing to do with the Bomb Squad.'

Water gurgled overhead and the landlord nodded en-couragingly. 'That'll be Doris taking care of your young lady.'

Mallory came on the line. 'Look, don't worry about it, Raven. The Bomb Squad doesn't have to know about the bank until afterwards. I'll pass the word on as a tip from an informer.'

I was less confident than he was. 'Suppose the Rat-catcher decides to check the Daimler and sees soldiers crawling all over it!'

'You worry too much,' he said impatiently. 'Burns is a pro. He's not going to be walking around *looking* for trouble. He'll be sitting somewhere safe waiting for the right moment. Where exactly is the bank?'

'Stanhope Gate, across from the Dorchester.' With the

explosions synchronised, the Ratcatcher wouldn't be able to hear the car go up in any case.

'And you've no idea of zero hour. Can't you make those bastards talk?'

Jimbo's eyes met mine in the mirror. 'Useless,' I said. Then the answer flashed. 'The car, of course. There's bound to be some sort of timing-device in the Daimler. The Bomb Boys would know from that!'

'Good thinking,' he said quickly. 'I'll ask them to defuse and leave the car where it is if they can. There's no guarantee. They may have to blow it up from remote control.'

'Do what you can,' I hurried. I was anxious to be on my way. 'What happens with this pair of jokers I've collected?'

'I've already talked to Medway. All you do is leave them with the locals. How long will it take you to get here?'

I challenged the landlord. 'Where can I get a car?'

His fat face creased with importance. 'There's one in the yard you can borrow.'

'I'm on my way as soon as the law arrives,' I told Mallory. 'Wait for me at the entrance to the Casualty Department, St George's Hospital.'

'O.K.,' he answered. 'By the way, our friend Drake is sniffing around.'

'*Drake?*' The name crawled like a worm in my brain. 'How do you mean he's sniffing around?'

'Don't shout,' he chided. 'All I know is that he's asked Control for an hourly fix on my two cars. Maybe he's psychic or something.'

My stomach plummeted. 'Jesus *God*! So what happens now?'

He sounded pleased with himself. 'Nothing. He's getting his fixes but they're not the right ones. Don't forget Drake fucked up years ago. Nobody loves him any more, not even Control. Now hang up and get moving!'

I put the receiver down. A card on top of the cash-register said *No Credit, No Problems.* Carpenter's face was haggard in the firelight. His yellow hair hung over his eyes. He was staring at the picture of Olga. My feelings about him were mixed. He'd get lagged almost certainly, do a model stretch and come out convinced that society owed him something. I lit a cigarette and stuck it between Jimbo's lips. His clothes were gently steaming.

He switched the smoke to the corner of his mouth. 'You're not a bad feller. Pity I'm going to have to sue you. You sunk my boat and that's seventy-five grands' worth. Have you got that sort of money, Raven?'

'I'll rob a bank,' I said. About him at least my thoughts were precise.

I offered the pack to Carpenter. He pulled a smoke out with shaking fingers.

'A good lawyer will help,' I said. 'I'll give you a name before I go.'

The landlord uncocked the hammers of his shotgun, his voice carefully casual.

'At the Yard, were you then?'

The fire collapsed. The Doberman jumped, clamping down her stump of a tail.

'I used to be,' I said. 'I'm retired.' It sounds somehow better than resigned.

He pushed his hand out. 'I'm an ex-copper myself. Twenty-five years of it. Hampshire Constabulary. You're going to need some dry clothes.'

The noise of an arriving car restored the Doberman's confidence. She stood in front of the door, stiff-legged and head low. The landlord snapped the leash on her collar and turned the key. Three uniformed cops pushed in led by a sergeant with a grey-moss moustache and a broken-veined nose. He peeled off his gloves and tucked them inside his overcoat.

'Which one of you's Raven?'

I tapped myself on the chest. 'Nice goings-on for a respectable riverside pub,' he said, wagging his head.

'Shut the bloody door,' said the landlord. He pointed at Jimbo and Carpenter. 'Villains from London.'

'Ah,' said the sergeant. 'I heard. Medway's been on. I can't accept him like that,' he said, looking disapprovingly at Jimbo.

'Pity,' said Jimbo.

'Watch him,' I warned. 'They're going to throw the key away for this one and he knows it.'

I unfastened the life-jacket. Jimbo flexed his arms and sneezed. The two constables moved in to flank him. Carpenter looked up from the snapshot at the sound of my voice, the ash long on his cigarette.

'What's the bank manager's telephone number?'

He gave it to me together with an address on Kensington High Street. I noted the details on a pad on the bar, scribbled a name on another sheet and gave it to him.

'Patrick O'Callaghan. Tell him the truth. He's about the best young criminal lawyer in the business.'

He stuffed the piece of paper in a pocket of his sodden suede jacket.

'Listen,' I said on impulse. 'You're going to be locked up with Burns and this other joker. And they're going to be telling you just how smart they are – how you can walk away from all this a free man and make a monkey out of everyone. It won't work, Carpenter. Your only out is the truth.'

The sergeant put his cap on. 'Who's signing the charge-sheet?'

'There'll be someone down tomorrow,' I said. 'In the meantime, keep them apart.'

The door behind the bar opened and Teresa came in, her long dark hair tied behind her ears. She was wearing a kimono at least three sizes too big for her and looked about seventeen. Her eyes were oddly searching as they met mine. The sergeant winked at the landlord's wife.

'Nice respectable house you keep here, Doris!' He nudged the pair by the fire to their feet.

Jimbo smiled cheerfully. 'I'll see you in court then, Raven. I'll be the one with the honest face.'

'Get that bugger outside,' growled the sergeant. 'And put the cuffs on the pair of them. Tomorrow then.' He lifted his hand in salute.

The door closed and the police car pulled away. The bar was suddenly quiet and peaceful. Teresa was standing by the fire, her fingers playing with the gold cross around her neck.

'How about those clothes?' asked the landlord. 'Come on upstairs with me and we'll find you something.'

'I'll keep my own, I think, thanks all the same. They're pretty nearly dry.' I was still watching Teresa.

'There's a bed for your girl if she wants it,' the landlord's wife said quickly. 'No sense now in her going out in the cold after what she's been through.'

'No sense at all,' I said. I crossed to the fireplace,

tipped Teresa's face in my hands and kissed her on the cheek. 'I'll see you tomorrow. Try to get a good night's sleep.'

She nodded slowly, a small girl at the end of a very long day. 'You are very brave, John.'

'I'm obstinate,' I corrected. 'It isn't the same thing.'

She caught my sleeve with her hand. For a moment I thought she was going to pull down my head and whisper in my ear. The seconds stretched and the spell finally broke.

'Look after yourself,' she said quietly.

'I'll try,' I said.

And now she did whisper. 'Yes, try.'

The landlady's motherly presence collected her. 'Don't you worry about her, now. She's in good hands.'

Her husband took the flashlight from the bar. The brickwork outside was drying in the rising wind under a fitful moon. He stared out across the river, his voice thoughtful. There was a hint of nostalgia in his tone, a memory of other times.

'Port of London Authority'll have to know about that boat sinking, just as soon as possible. There's regulations about things like that.'

'You could help me out,' I suggested. 'You could get on to the river police and let them know what's happened. She's lying more or less in line with the steps about five hundred yards out.'

'I could do that all right.' His fat face brightened. 'I'll get in touch with them right away.'

The vast courtyard was a throwback to coaching days with stables and mounting-blocks. Lights twinkled far beyond the end wall. It was a lonely spot and he seemed at that moment to feel it.

'This'll be a real big one, I'll lay.'

'It's big but I can't talk about it,' I said. 'I know you'll understand.'

He nodded, touching his nose with his finger. 'Mum's the word.'

He unlocked double doors on the last sort of car I expected to see. It was an early-model Thunderbird in mint condition, white with gleaming chrome. He patted the front affectionately.

'There's enough petrol to take you to London. You can bring her back tomorrow when you come to fetch your girl. And take care on the corners, she's inclined to run away with you.'

I put myself behind the wheel and adjusted the seat. There was plenty of room for my legs, a stack of tapes for the cassette player. He leaned in, smelling comfortably of beer and woodsmoke.

'Ah,' he said. 'Take you anywhere, she will.'

I knew that he longed to be in the driver's seat or at least a passenger.

'She's not my girl, incidentally.'

He showed me his thumb and winked. 'That's not what she thinks. Cheerioh, then and mind – there's only a few of us left.'

I turned the ignition key. The powerful motor responded immediately. I backed out of the yard with him fussing like a bird whose chick takes its first flight. The weather had changed completely. It was quite dry though the moon was hidden. I put my foot down and the car shot across the clearing in front of the pub. I drove with the memory of Teresa's face peering out of the taproom window. She was a world apart from the sort of girls I'd been squiring lately and her interest flattered me. I don't suppose anyone will ever replace Cathy but it's a pity.

CHAPTER ELEVEN

The big headlamps ate into the windy darkness, the telephone-poles rushing back at sixty miles an hour. The oil pressure was steady and the battery charging. There was nothing to do but drive and think. I thought of Drake. Our relationship was becoming an obsession. Nobody else seemed to realise what was going on in his mind. He'd seemed no more than bad news when we'd met again in Chelsea police station. But I understood now that he had never forgotten me, not for one single day. My crime was to have beaten him at his own game, playing his rules, and it was more than he could endure. It didn't seem to matter to him that he was a senior-ranking policeman. He had an implacable will to revenge, a desire to destroy and complicate my life and this justified my own stand. Stripped of the trimmings, the struggle was basic between Drake and me. And he had to be beaten again and again, if necessary, until he finally admitted defeat. It worried me to think that he might have nosed out the Ratcatcher caper as a buzzard scents carrion.

Hard driving brought me to Deptford. I cut across into the black ghettoes of Camberwell. It was getting on for midnight but music was snapping from lighted doorways and soul-brothers strutted in front of the High Life Social Club. The politicians can say what they like but I feel that this is no longer my country. I know it not to be so. Strobe lights were running colour over the stretches of drying pavement. Wax-models turned an endless display of cheap fashions to empty streets.

I chose Vauxhall Bridge, skirting the late-night squalor of Victoria Station, down Eccleston Street and into Belgrave Square. I parked a hundred yards away from St George's Hospital. There was no sign of Mallory's Jaguar. My watch was useless but the clock on the dash said ten minutes after midnight. A lighted box over the semi-circular portico identified the entrance to the Casualty Department. I couldn't have made a mistake.

St George's Hospital serves the more sensitive areas of the West End, catching its share of the weekend rough-house trade. There's always a steady stream of ambulances arriving on Friday and Saturday nights, paralytic drunks, the victims of accident and assault, the lonely and troubled in spirit pushed to the extremity of suicide. I'd spent quite a few hours there in the old days, waiting at bedsides, filling in forms, listening to doctors. It's a place of complete anonymity where patient and visitor alike are reduced to a scribble on a card. I locked the Thunderbird and walked east towards Hyde Park Corner. As I neared the Casualty entrance something prompted me to look beneath the portico. The Jaguar was parked just inside in the driveway with Mallory at the wheel talking to Jerry Soo. Their heads turned in unison as I rapped on the back window. I climbed in behind them.

Mallory closed his eyes, looked at my clothes and shut them again. My trousers had dried in corrugated ridges and green slime was pasted into my sweater. The lump over my ear was still tender and I knew that my hair was a crowsnest.

'O.K.,' I said. 'So you expected Beau Brummel. How much time have we got?'

Mallory's hands appeared from under his green cloak and he picked the end of his nose.

'About three-quarters of an hour. The Daimler was parked outside the Christian Science Church. Some hero defused it. The thing was timed to go off at twelve-forty-five.'

'Did they take the car away?'

He shook his head. 'They left it. It was touch-and-go for a while. I take my hat off to those people. There were no questions. I told them I'd had this tip and they accepted it. We were lucky we had the military to deal with.'

A man with his eye cupped in a bloodstained hand staggered by supported by a weeping woman.

Jerry Soo shook his head. 'I wish you wouldn't get me out like this. I abhor mindless violence.'

'You bet,' said Mallory. 'We're depraved and decadent and it makes you feel superior.'

I gave him the bank manager's telephone number. 'What do we need him for?' he asked suspiciously. 'I mean *now*.'

'Why not?' I challenged. 'It seems to me to be logical.'

'The fuck it is,' said Mallory. 'This joker's going to be more interested in saving his bank from being blown up than copping the Ratcatcher. And the book's on his side, remember. We're supposed to be scouring the city, preventing crime.'

I nodded agreement. It made sense. 'In other words we don't even know the name of the bank until about fifty minutes from now.'

'I'd say nearer forty.' Mallory closed his right eye.

'The result of good intelligent police-work. My second car's in Berkeley Square.'

A man in a white coat left the lighted office and came across to us.

'You're going to have to move now. I can't let you stay any longer. I need the space for the ambulances.'

'We're on our way,' said Mallory. 'With any luck you won't see us again.' He engaged gear and moved the Jaguar into the freeforall of Hyde Park Corner.

We turned left out of Piccadilly, up Park Street and into Stanhope Gate. Nobody's head turned as we cruised past the bank but I saw it in the rearview mirror, a new building inside an old one, steel and concrete reinforcing the elegant seventeenth-century façade. The massive bronze doors were modern and adorned with friezes of Saluki hounds hunting gazelles. Lights shone in the first floor windows but the upper floors were in darkness.

Mallory spoke from the side of his mouth. 'How many entrances are there?'

'Only the one.' It required an effort not to turn and stare openly. 'Do you think he's in there?'

Jerry suspended his ginseng chewing. 'You can bet your arse on it. He'll need time to set things up. He's padding around in there quite sure of himself.'

Traffic was heavy coming south on Park Lane. People were on their way home from theatre and restaurant. Beyond the park railings a hint of moon illuminated scarecrow trees and deserted walks. Mallory put his foot down hard. I grabbed the arm-rest as the heavy car shot towards the fountains in front of the Dorchester. Mallory eased in after an emerging taxi, stopped the motor and cut the lights.

161

'Here he comes,' he said as a doorman in a tophat bustled across officiously.

'Excuse me, sir. Are you staying in the hotel?'

'Can't afford it,' said Mallory.

'Then I'm afraid you can't park here, sir. This space is reserved for guests.'

'I'm a ratepayer,' said Mallory. 'Here, look!' He flashed the warrant-card in the palm of his hand. 'Piss off and leave us alone.'

We were obliquely across from the bank, a hundred yards or so from the entrance. Mallory used his radiophone. The second car appeared almost immediately, turning in at the far end of Stanhope Gate and stopping there.

The driver flashed his headlamps briefly. Mallory sucked on the match in the corner of his mouth.

'Who wants to bet which way he goes when he comes out? You can have an even pound.'

'A few minutes' work and all that money,' said Jerry, looking through the windshield at the lighted bank.

His breath smelled of the root he was chewing. I leaned forward, following his gaze.

'You're forgetting the training. All those years spent eating porridge not to mention the chance of getting your arms and legs blown off. And in any case you don't *get* your money. You wind up sewing mailbags for the rest of your life.'

Mallory opened the glove-compartment and produced a couple of police thirty-eights. He checked the cylinders and placed one in Soo's lap.

'I forged your signature. If you fire the fucking thing they'll want another so be careful. And remember about the safety-catch.'

I leaned forward and touched his shoulder. 'How about me? Don't I get one?'

He half-slewed in his seat. 'This is for the boys in blue. You're only a bloody civilian.'

He was edgy in spite of his show of confidence. It showed in the way he drummed his fingers on the steering wheel. As far as I was concerned he had every reason to be nervous. Busting the Ratcatcher was about as safe a venture as tickling a king cobra. Jerry was unmoved, his solid reliable self, his voice reasonable as he spoke over his shoulder.

'If there's trouble, John, you keep out of it. O.K?'

I lifted a hand in assent. They were both sticking their necks out for me but Jerry's motive was friendship. The least I could do was respect his wishes. The hotel entrance was immediately behind us. I could see through into the crowded foyer. People were drinking nightcaps, involved in animated conversation. Cars arrived from the airport. Other guests were checking out. Yet a couple of hundred yards away a man was preparing to steal half-a-million pounds.

We were sitting in absolute darkness except for the glow of the clock on the dash. The Ratcatcher's timing would have been synchronised with the device in the Daimler. I thought of asking Mallory if he'd set his own watch accordingly but his manner discouraged conversation. He was sitting well back in his seat, intent on the bank entrance. It was Jerry who asked the questions. I told him how I'd found Teresa and Carpenter, described how we'd escaped from the boat. It seemed that he'd gone to Tregunter Road to discover that Teresa had left with Carpenter late in the afternoon. He'd driven to Paddington, hung around in the pub as

163

arranged till it closed and then contacted Mallory. For some obscure reason he'd remembered the number of the Ratcatcher's house but not the street.

Mallory lifted his hands from the wheel with sudden violence. 'For God's sake! "Then I did this and he did that!" I'm trying to concentrate on a bank robbery!'

My breathing was loud in the sudden silence. I think it was mine. It could have been Mallory's. I knew that I needed a drink and I didn't want him to miss any of what I intended to say.

'I'd advise you to keep a civil tongue in your head. I don't have to put up with your crap. If you're nervous suck your thumb.'

He glanced up at the rearview mirror and then grinned. 'I'm sorry. It's the waiting that does it. I've never been good at waiting.'

There were two cigarettes left in the pack. I'd bought them in the Pakistani corner shop what seemed like a lifetime ago.

'What about Trinny – the guy who was chauffeuring the Daimler?'

Jerry answered for him. 'Big, bad and black. We tried Intelligence and C.R.O. Nobody seems to recognise the name and description.'

I flicked ash at the floor carpet. 'I'd say that he's planted by now. He knows too much.'

Mallory tipped his hat back, his eyes never leaving the bank entrance. 'And I'd say you're right. The Ratcatcher never took prizes for good behaviour and there's half-a-million quid at stake.'

I gave him the passport I'd found on the boat. He held it close to the glow from the clock, flicking through the pages. Then he stuffed it in the glove-compartment.

'*Brazil*, the bastard!'

'He'd never have made it,' I said. 'We're doing him a favour. Jimbo was going to sink him with the rest of us.'

A couple of young men swung in from Park Lane wearing Scott Fitzgerald caps and woollen scarves bright with club-colours. They swayed across the courtyard, peering at the line of parked cars. One of them fluttered his fingers as he passed. Mallory's head lifted and the taller of the two tittered. His voice fluted back as they hurried across the street.

'The *shame* of it! Me trying to get off with Old Bill!'

Mallory snarled and Jerry winked. 'It takes all sorts.'

The minute-hand on the clock crept round. Twelve-forty. Twelve-forty-six. The explosion was a lot quieter than I had expected. It started with a low rumble like an underground train coming into a station. A deep muffled sound followed, rattling the windows. The lights in the bank flickered then steadied again. I heard someone shout and looked through the back window at the hotel entrance. The people who had been waiting for cabs were milling around like ants disturbed in their nest. A car pulled away hurriedly. One of the tophatted doormen pointed in the wrong direction. No one seemed to be sure what had happened let alone where or why. The Park Lane traffic continued to roll south. Whatever had been seen or heard would soon be forgotten.

There was nothing in Stanhope Gate except the police car parked at the far end. Mallory looked at his watch, his stringy neck working.

'It'll take him five minutes to clear the vaults. Five minutes at least.'

Jerry was sitting bolt upright beside him, beaming his square smile through the windshield. I watched the bronze doors as the minutes lengthened. Mallory picked up the radiophone, covering his mouth as he spoke.

'He'll be coming out any moment now. Remember, the bastard's dangerous. Don't take chances.'

He pulled the catch back on his door in readiness. He was whistling *Abide With Me* loud enough to hear that he was flat. Ten minutes went by. Five to one by the clock. Jerry voiced what all three of us were thinking.

'Something must have gone wrong.'

Mallory straightened up, shaking his head. 'I make it sixteen minutes.'

My own feeling was that the Ratcatcher had touched himself off with the gelignite. He was an old hand at the game but the slightest miscalculation was the difference between success and disaster. I said so.

Mallory thought for a moment and reached back over his shoulder. 'Where's that bank manager's address?'

I put the slip of paper in his palm. He used the phone again, talking to the Duty Officer in his section.

'Phillimore Court, Kensington High Street. Get someone over there right away. Mr El Hami. Tell him his bank's just been burgled. We're parked in front of the Dorchester. *Move!*'

He hung up and looked at a blood-bruise on his thumbnail, shaking his head.

'I don't believe it. That sod would never blow himself up.'

I looked at Soo's stocky back. 'Jerry?'

His shoulders rose and fell. 'If there's only one way out of the place he's still in there, alive or dead. I suppose it's just possible that he's waiting to be collected.'

'Then they're going to find him plastered all over the ceiling,' I said.

Mallory spoke to the other car. 'Something's gone wrong in there. The keys are on their way. As soon as they arrive we go in. I want two of you covering both ends of the street. The driver stays put. O.K?'

He put the phone back and checked his watch yet again. 'I could have been in a nice warm bed discussing Ugandan affairs with a lady of my acquaintance. There's got to be a moral there somewhere.'

'A boy's best friend is his mother?' I suggested. He was getting on my nerves and I was down to my last cigarette.

We sat with our ears on stalks, listening for the first sound of the squad-car. It seemed to appear from nowhere, peeling off from the stream of southbound traffic, two-tone alarm going, blue light flashing. It stopped in front of the fountains and the doors flew open. Two plain clothes men hustled a slightly-built Arab towards us. They let him go as they reached the Jaguar. He stood there looking bewilderedly through spectacles.

'Oriental charm and diplomacy,' muttered Jerry and padded out on bandy legs. There was a short conversation in which Mallory joined. I saw the Arab hand over keys. Jerry walked him back to the Jaguar, winking on the Arab's blind side.

'This gentleman's not feeling too well, John. Take care of him.' He rejoined Mallory. They crossed the street towards the bank with the Arab's escort.

The bank manager put his hand on my sleeve. His voice was deep and resonant with a great deal of glottal stopping.

'I do not understand, sir. Who robbing the bank?

What is the meaning of this outrage? I am Kuwaiti subject!'

'I'll talk to you later,' I said and opened the door. I reached the group outside the bank as Mallory put the first key in the massive bronze doors. There were three locks and his fingers were clumsy. Somebody pulled the curtains in the second-floor apartment across the street. An elderly woman wearing a shawl appeared at the window, watching the proceedings with interest. She was the sort of person you'd have expected to be in bed. If ever *she* decided to call the police Stanhope Gate would be a three-ring circus.

Jerry stepped back as the doors opened. For once he wasn't smiling. He looked strange with the gun in his hand.

'Why didn't you stay in the car?'

'I just didn't hear you,' I said.

The stink of exploded gelignite hung in the air. The marble floor was covered with a layer of powdered glass and pulverised plaster. The same fine powdering covered the steps leading down to the vaults. Mallory signalled the others to follow and led the way below, holding his gun stiff-armed. The woman across the street could see directly into the banking hall. Her face was a study in amazement.

The counter was protected by bandit-proof glass, the manager's office reached through a door at the far end. Suddenly I noticed faint marks in the dust on the vault stairs, near the banister. Someone had come from the basement after the dust had settled. I glanced right automatically. A passage at the other end of the counter led to the rear of the premises. The acrid smell of an explosion grew stronger as I moved along the passage.

I turned the corner to face a door drooping on broken hinges. Inside the store-room was total confusion. The contents of shelves had been hurled against the walls. Typing-paper, chequebooks, ledgers. Ink and boxes of clips. Some of the objects were embedded in one another, others were deep in the plaster. A hole large enough to let through a small car gaped in the party-wall to the adjoining building.

CHAPTER TWELVE

The Ratcatcher's plan had been more sophisticated than any of us had realised. It called for three explosions, not two, all timed to go off at the same moment. Once the vaults were open, Burns had grabbed what he wanted, stepped through the hole in the storeroom wall and walked out into Curzon Street. It would have killed me to laugh but it was what I felt like doing.

I could hear Mallory shouting down below, the noise echoing through the shattered wall in front of me. There was a glimmer of light beyond the rubble, an open door and some travel-posters, a lifesize cutout of an airline hostess. I climbed through into a travel agency, reading its title on a window backwards: *Merlin Travel Service*.

The desire to laugh was even stronger. The Ratcatcher's escape door opened no more than fifty yards away from Park Lane, a hundred or so from Piccadilly. He'd have emerged, an inconspicuous figure to be swallowed up by the night. The Daimler was too far along Curzon Street for him to have seen it from the travel agency. But even if he'd gone in that direction, he could only have thought that the charge had failed to explode. The rest of his scheme had worked, one botched element meant nothing.

I crawled back through the hole and ran along the passage shouting for the others. They were coming up the stairs from the vaults, their clothes grey with dust. Mallory had dirt on his face.

I looked at him with a strange sense of euphoria. They might be finished but I wasn't.

'He's gone,' I said. 'Blown through to the next building and walked out into Curzon Street.'

Mallory's face reddened. '*Shit!*' He banged the plaster from his hat furiously. His top denture shifted with the force of emotion. 'I knew that bastard was too smart to die. Wait till you see downstairs. He's picked off those vault doors like a cat taking fish off the bone!'

The thought seemed to infuriate him still more. He swung round on the trio of detectives behind him.

'What the fuck are you standing there for? Why doesn't one of you *do* something? Somebody fetch that wog from the car!'

He pulled his hat down on his head. The dirt was still on his face. He looked like a bull in a ring, tormented from every side, unsure where to charge. He picked on the woman in the window across the street.

'Look at her!' he denounced. 'If she'd had her bloody nose there when the Ratcatcher opened the bank up it might have been some use. *Get inside!*' There was no chance of the woman hearing him but he advanced across the hall, waving his arms and muttering.

The bank manager appeared, flanked by the two plain clothesmen. He stood stockstill in the entrance, hands clasped, surveying the surrounding wreckage.

'I must telephone my embassy,' he said harshly. 'These are disaster.'

'Never mind the embassy.' Mallory jerked his hand in Soo's direction. 'Go with this officer and make a list of whatever's missing.'

The Arab's face was stricken. 'Disaster,' he repeated. Jerry Soo took him by the arm.

'What's he mean, disaster?' Mallory said sourly, looking after the bank manager. 'They've got all the money left in the world, haven't they?'

'Documents?' I suggested. 'Oil treaties. Who knows with these people?'

He hit his forehead hard with the heel of his hand. 'What are you doing in here anyway? You're supposed to be outside in the car.'

'I know what I'm supposed to be doing,' I answered. 'Take a look at this.'

He followed me down the passage to the blasted storeroom, shaking his head as he saw the hole in the wall. We climbed over the rubble into the neighbouring building. He found what I'd missed in the travel agency, a burglar alarm switch concealed behind an exotic poster. He opened the street-door looking up at the bell overhead. It was silent. He shut the door again and nodded morosely.

'The bastard seems to have thought of everything.'

Ironically enough, the poster portrayed Brazilian beaches, a suntanned man under a parasol and what could have been the girl from Ipinima.

'You're wrong,' I said. 'He hasn't thought of everything. He's only got one way of getting out of the country and as far as he's concerned the whole system is go. I know where he's supposed to meet the boat. The time and the place.'

'And you're not going to tell me?' His nose had gone dead white against the ruddiness of his cheeks.

'When I'm good and ready,' I said, meeting his look head-on.

'I could do you for it,' he threatened. 'What is this, anyway – some sort of blackmail?'

A couple went by on the pavement. The man turned his face curiously as he passed, staring in at us.

'Call it what you like,' I said. 'But I haven't come this far to sit in a car and hold someone's hand. That wasn't the deal.'

'It *is* blackmail,' he answered in a tight voice. 'You're obstructing a police officer in pursuit of his duty.'

'Fiddle!' I said. 'All I know is that you haven't a hope of busting Burns without me.'

People on the Flying Squad have a reputation of being hard-nosed. It must have needled him to be picked up and have his face wiped. The corners of his mouth twitched into a sort of smile.

'I know the deal *I* made. What was yours?'

'It's simple enough. No one's patting me on the back and sending me home. I'm staying to the end.'

He moved his head up and down. 'I should have known it. How much time have we got?'

I gave him gesture for gesture. 'Enough.'

The others were waiting in the marble hall, the bank manager grey-faced beside Jerry.

'What's the damage?' asked Mallory.

The Arab's wave took in the dust-dimmed lights, the steel doors sagging at the bottom of the stairs. They'd been blown from their concrete beds with such force that fragments of steel had gouged out great chunks of the ceiling.

'Is he daft?' muttered Mallory. 'Not that— How much money have you lost?'

The manager read from the paper in his hand. 'Seven hundred, thirty-five thousand United States dollars.

Three hundred eighty thousand Deutschmarks. Two hundred sixty-four thousand Swiss francs. The sterling was in the end vault. Not touched.'

Mallory glanced up from the notes he was making. 'He probably didn't have time. How much is that in pounds, approximately?'

The Arab's guttural voice gave the answer emphasis. 'At today's rates about four hundred ninety thousand pounds.'

Mallory and Soo exchanged glances. Jerry suspended his chewing for a moment.

'A profitable night's work. Apparently there were securities in the end vault as well as the sterling.'

'The thieves are knowing what they are doing,' put in the manager.

'Experts,' Mallory said shortly. 'How much space would this money occupy?'

Mr El Hami's slim fingers built a box in the air. Mallory snapped his notebook shut.

'A large suitcase and he wouldn't have wanted to carry it far. He must have had a car parked somewhere nearby.'

The manager came to life. 'You know the robbers?' he asked hopefully.

'We know.' Mallory put an arm round the Arab's shoulders, looking like a large green cat with a small brown mouse in its mouth. 'I'm sending you home in a car. Try to get some sleep. We'll lock up here and be in touch first thing in the morning.'

'There are things I must do,' the Arab objected. 'I must notify my embassy, my staff.'

I interrupted for the first time. 'You can forget about

one of your staff. Someone called Paul Carpenter. He's in this up to his ears.'

He was too stunned even to show surprise. Mallory crooked a finger at a couple of plain clothes men.

'Drive this gentleman home. The rest of you hang about till the fingerprint people get here. For what good *that's* going to be.'

It was fresh outside with the wind whipping across the park from the north. I pointed across at the lighted façade of the hotel.

'I won't be a moment. I need cigarettes.'

Mallory's look mocked me. 'You wouldn't get past the door dressed like that. In the car.'

The bank doors were shut, the crew of the squad car moving on the late-night curious.

'Don't let him worry you,' Jerry said quietly. 'Just take it easy.'

'I don't *have* to worry about him,' I said obstinately. 'He's the one who has to worry.'

Mallory was back to drop a couple of packs of cigarettes in my lap. He was observant. They were my brand.

'Compliments of the Flying Squad,' he said, poker-faced. He picked up the phone, organised the Finger-print Squad and asked for yet another extension. 'Answer yes or no – is the Beast still about?' He put the receiver down and winked. 'Drake's gone home. How about you, Jerry. You want to get your head down?'

Jerry's eyes were almost lost in his wide smile. 'And lose my share of that fat reward? You must be joking.'

It was nonsense and we all knew it. A cop's reward is his pay-packet. It came to me suddenly that if the bank rewarded anyone it would have to be me.

Mallory tapped the face of his watch with a fingernail. 'It's twenty past one. It's up to you, Raven. Where's our next stop?'

'Have you got any maps?' I asked. 'I need a large-scale map of Essex.'

He jerked a thumb at the pile on the ledge behind me. 'The one with the black cover.' There was a legend across the front. H.M. CUSTOMS & EXCISE. DO NOT REMOVE. Mallory moved a shoulder. 'We're working for the same company.'

The ordnance-maps were a cartographer's dream, printed on linen and folded so that any given field might be reduced to a single four-inch square. The course of the River Crouch was faithfully drawn, its width and depth clearly marked. Houses and churches were identified, even some farm-buildings. The creek designated as the Ratcatcher's rendezvous flowed due south. The vertical strokes on the east indicated marshland. There was a tiny oblong near the mouth of the creek which had to be the jetty Jimbo had spoken about.

Mallory and Jerry leaned back as I traced the way the river ran. 'This is where he expects the boat to come in. You can see for yourselves. There are no roads anywhere near. A car would have to be left somewhere *here*.' I pointed at the huddle of buildings shown in the hamlet. The creek and the jetty were a good two miles away.

Mallory made a grumbling noise deep in his throat. 'I don't get it. There must be dozens of places along this coast where he could have stepped straight on to a boat from a car. Why trudge over ploughed fields carrying a heavy suitcase?'

Jerry's manner took on the diffidence he assumes when he thinks he sees a flaw in someone else's chess game.

'I can see why. The sort of place you're talking about people tend to know one another. They're conscious of strangers, especially in winter. All it needs is someone up to take a leak. He looks through the window and along comes the Ratcatcher at three o'clock in the morning and, as you say, carrying a heavy suitcase. No, it has to be somewhere isolated.'

I refolded the map and put it back with the others. I had a sudden vision of the Ratcatcher, goggled and anonymous, riding a machine with panniers stuffed with loot.

'Suppose he's using a motorcycle,' I suggested.

Mallory eased his shirt-collar with his thumb, frowning. 'It's a thought,' said Jerry.

Mallory's look was exasperated. 'I'm getting pissed off with all this peekaboo stuff. Why do you have to turn everything into a mystery, Raven?'

'I'm getting pissed off with both of you,' Jerry retorted, suddenly squarefaced and serious. 'A villain's on his way with half-a-million pounds' worth of foreign currency and you're acting like children.'

Mallory switched on the ignition. 'How far is this place?'

'About thirty-five miles,' I said. 'Straight up the A127. We turn off at Rayleigh.'

He shaved his chin with a forefinger, frowning. 'He'll need a change of clothes.'

'He's got one,' I answered. 'At least he thinks he has. On the boat.'

He let in the clutch. 'I'm going to take another look at that house.'

We streaked north into the wilds of Paddington. The pubs were closed but lights blinked outside a couple of late-night drinking-places. Swallow Street was a row of quiet darkened houses in contrast to the lively vulgarity behind us. The Jaguar ghosted to the far end of the street and stopped. Mallory used his radiophone. A couple of men left the other car and disappeared towards the backs of the houses, a third stationed himself on the pavement. Mallory pulled the gun from his pocket, shaking his head as Jerry started to follow.

'No, you cover me. If he's there and makes a run for it, hit him anywhere below the belly button.'

He moved along the railings, the shadow cast by the street lamp preceding him. The clatter of the doorknocker sounded along the sleeping street. Mallory hit it again. Dogs started to bark from all directions. Mallory stepped back from the doorway, looking up at the curtained windows. Lights came on in the neighbouring house. A man's head appeared, his face contorted with fury.

'Don't you bloody people have any respect for others? This is the third time we've been woken up in as many nights. I'm calling the police. *Now!*'

'We *are* the police,' called Mallory. 'Go back to bed.' He climbed behind the steering wheel. 'It was a chance.'

We waited till the plain clothes men had returned to the other car. I could see the Ratcatcher's neighbour taking down the numbers of both vehicles.

CHAPTER THIRTEEN

We were in Rayleigh in fifty-two minutes. The Jaguar turned north, leading the way into a network of narrow lanes. The heavy rain had soaked the countryside. Freshets gushed from the sodden banks. Our wheels sprayed water into the beam of the headlamps. After six or seven miles the narrow road climbed to a rise on the south bank of the Crouch. It came to an end, circling a village green and running back on itself. There were half-a-dozen houses, all shut tight for the night. Enormous elms surrounded the green, yellowed and dying, doomed by the Dutch disease.

A bleached, faded sign hung outside a deserted weatherboard inn. Mallory put his foot on the brake. Our lights shone down over sloping grass to the rotting hulks of sailboats and the glimmer of water. On our right was a ruined ragstone church with a Charles Addams vicarage attached, overgrown by unkempt rhododendron bushes. Mallory signalled the other car to follow. We whispered on to the vicarage driveway. Broken glass littered the tangled flowerbeds and the front door lay toppled in its framework. A dank smell hung in the air as if the vicarage had at one time been drowned.

Mallory disappeared to unlock the boot. He came back with a pair of binoculars, clambered up on the base of a toppled statue and trained them across the flat expanse of fields to the east. He beckoned me over to join him.

'See what you make of it.' The night-glasses were stamped with the Luftwaffe insignia. Visibility was fair, the low cloud ceiling had lifted. Powerful lens drew the scene close. I could see the thick clumps of reeds along the river bank, straight furrows where winter wheat had been sown.

The reeds marked the course of the creek behind what looked like a barn. I refocused and held the image till I was able to distinguish movement, the outline of black and white shapes.

'A cowshed,' I said promptly. 'There are cattle in there.'

He showed no wish to investigate further. I gave him the binoculars and walked back to the Jaguar. He let me in beside Jerry and leaned against the door from outside, talking through the open window.

'There's only one footpath marked, right?'

I shrugged. 'The map's twelve years old. The contour of the fields could have changed since then.'

'Is that right?' he said, cocking his face on one side.

'What's the difference?' Jerry broke in quickly.

'There's one footpath,' Mallory repeated. 'It goes straight down the middle of those two fields by the river – at the side of the hedge. If Burns is riding a motorcycle there'll be tyre-marks.'

Jerry nodded at the surrounding shadows. 'There's no place he could have left a car, that's for sure.'

Mallory pushed off the door. His manner betrayed no hint of nervousness.

'I'm going to take a look.' He picked his way through the dank shrubbery, past the other car and vanished in the direction of the green. Something behind us clanked in the wind. I turned sharply, scanning the front of the ruined vicarage. I had a presentiment of being watched.

Jerry unfolded his arms. 'Relax, John. You're letting this thing get on top of you.'

He drowned me in his customary smile as though to reassure me of his understanding. Yet he didn't *seem* to understand. This was a matter between the Rat-catcher and me and I had the inner certainty that I had his measure. I *needed* no one else, least of all Mallory and his sniping. If I could have had my way I'd have had the lot of them home in their beds.

'Don't worry about me, Jerry,' I said. 'I'm all right.'

His teeth gleamed white in the half-light. 'With some-one like you who can help worrying?'

The wind was chasing through the empty rooms and corridors of the vicarage. I could see the glow of cigar-ettes in the other car. The five men there were locked in their own silent world. All eyes were fixed on the shrubbery, at the point through which Mallory had gone. He reappeared, trotting – long green overcoat flap-ping, hat on the back of his head, his trousers stuffed into his socks. He rested his arms on the roof of the Jaguar, breathing heavily.

'He's there all right *and* on a motorcycle. You can see where he's been. There are tyre and skid marks all over the pathway.'

The hedgerows ran due east to the creek, about half-a-mile away. Beyond the creek lay the marshes. There were three gates to negotiate but the Ratcatcher could have ridden as far as the landing stage and simply drowned his machine in the water.

Mallory mopped his forehead, leaning his body sideways and blocking me from the conversation.

'Over half-an-hour to go before the boat's supposed to arrive. What do you think, Jerry?'

'About what?' Jerry asked quietly.

'That bastard out there. What do you think he's up to?'

I heard Jerry's teeth bite on his ginseng root. 'He's supposed to be a psychopath. I'm not too sure what that is. But you only have to look at his record. Assault with a deadly weapon. Grievous Bodily Harm. Possession of Explosives.'

'And sitting on half-a-million pounds,' I said. Neither of them seemed to hear me.

'I know his record,' Mallory said twitchily. The trip into the fields had destroyed his equanimity. 'He's done that spade for a certainty. He's not going to give himself up.'

As far as I was concerned it was self-evident. Trinny would have driven Burns back in the Daimler. There'd been no traffic-wardens on duty. They'd simply parked the car packed with gelignite then walked away from it. The negro must have been killed between then and the Ratcatcher going into the bank.

'Twenty-five minutes.' Mallory turned his head, looking at me. 'If you hadn't been so bloody coy we could have had this place surrounded instead of putting six men's lives at risk.'

There was nothing ambiguous about his hostility and I met it head-on.

'What's the matter, things beginning to get to you, Mallory?'

He looked at me hard and then smiled. He seemed to lift his displeasure from me.

'We can be sure of one thing. He's not going to come to us.'

The surrounding trees bent and whistled, the lights five hundred yards across the river enhancing our wind-swept loneliness.

'He's had it all his own way up to now,' said Jerry. 'There's no reason he won't think it'll last. What's on his mind at this moment is the boat and the people he imagines are on it. And that's where he comes unstuck.'

'You mean sneak up on him?' asked Mallory.

Jerry moved diffidently. 'The longer it goes, the more wary he gets. I'd say take him now.'

'You're right,' said Mallory. He crossed to the second car. A couple of plain clothes men climbed out and walked off through the shrubbery. Mallory came back, peeling off his topcoat. He dropped it on the rear seat along with his hat. He'd picked up a walkie-talkie set from the other car. His trousers were still stuffed in his socks and he was holding his gun.

I was dead sure that they were wrong, all of them. They were cast in the mould of the city, playing the urban game of cops and robbers. It was no good treating this as the last street door to be kicked down. I tried to put it into words.

'He's an animal and he thinks like an animal. If he hasn't already sensed that we're here, he soon will.'

Mallory nodded in the direction the two cops had taken, talking to Jerry.

'They're going to hit the creek a couple of hundred yards down from the landing stage and work their way along the bank to the cowshed. One of them's a marks-man. The rest of us come up from behind.'

A voice crackled in the set on his chest. 'We're half-way there boss. The clump of trees you see on your right. No sign of anything yet. Out.'

Mallory poked his rawboned face at me. 'You and the driver are staying here. He's armed. If the Rat-catcher does slip through you've got the moment of glory you've been waiting for.'

'I'm staying here?' I could feel my voice beginning to shake. Jerry put his hand on my arm.

'You're staying,' said Mallory. 'I've had just about enough of you, one way and another. They said you were a troublemaker and they were right.'

Jerry eased out of his seat. 'Be reasonable, John. You're here. You've got what you asked for.'

'*Reasonable?*' It seemed an odd word to choose. But he was in the middle so to speak and I knew what he meant. 'Watch yourself, Jerry,' I said.

I waited till the four figures were out of sight then unfastened the door of the Jaguar. The driver of the second police car let me go five yards before pushing his head out of the window.

'Where do you think you're going?' he called.

I pointed ahead at the rhododendrons. 'What am I supposed to do, shove my hand up and ask for permission?'

I didn't give him any time to think but shouldered my way through the tangled overgrown bushes. As soon as I reached the green on the other side I started to run. I heard the driver floundering after me. I was already down by the weatherboard inn when he came in sight. He stood there for a moment, turning his head and sniffing like a fox. Then he started jogging back towards the cars. He was carrying a pistol in his right hand. I wondered whether he intended using it on me.

I tiptoed through the debris that littered the river bank. Quiet as I was, the village-green seemed to echo the sound of my footsteps, carrying them across the flat fields to waiting cars.

Boats had been hauled ashore and abandoned in matted grass and nettlebeds, others lay half-submerged among the rushes. I moved along the bank to a jetty behind the broken-down inn, spongy earth sucking my shoes. People in the area still ferried across the river. A small dinghy was tied to a post, the oars removed. There was an inch of rainwater lying under the seat but the hull looked sound. I picked a stave from a broken barrel, lowered myself into the dinghy and shoved it off. The ebbing tide was running fast under a ragged sky, carrying the boat towards the mouth of the creek a quarter of a mile away. I was using the barrel-stave as a rudder, steering as close to the bank as I could without getting snarled in the reeds and the roots of the bog-oaks. The river was alive with sounds of its own that I recognised. The startled quack of a duck, the plop of a water-vole, the haunting cry of an owl. The current grew stronger, sweeping the small dinghy near the clutching branches of the gaunt trees that straddled the overhanging bank.

I was using the stave as a paddle now, badly-balanced and trying to keep one eye on the bank. I could see the mouth of the creek and the outline of the cattle-shed. I steered into reeds that grew a good four feet above my head. The rustle of the boat's passage was lost in the overall noise of the river. A steer bellowed with startling suddenness. I located the animal no more than six yards away, standing kneedeep in water, drinking. The bank had been trampled down, a muddy path gouged by the herd of beasts. The bullock saw me and backed off, holding its head low and wrenching its feet out of the mud. Alders had been planted to prevent erosion and their roots were firmly entrenched in the heavy clay. I pulled the boat through the rushes and grabbed at an overhead branch, standing precariously. The branch took my weight and I swung, using my legs. I landed on all fours at the foot of an alder. The bullock snorted with fear and galloped off to the shelter. Another beast bellowed in sympathy then all was quiet again.

I lifted my head slowly, looking across at the cow-shelter. The landing stage was directly behind it and hidden. The Ratcatcher was somewhere over there but I could see no sign of him. I imagined him, aware of danger and probing the darkness for its source. I moved forward, using the alders as cover till I was abreast of the cattleshed. The bullocks were completely still. I heard the owl hoot again beyond the mist over the marshes. I was no more than a dozen yards from the shed now. I made it, stopping with each pace and looking round like a child playing a nursery game.

The bullocks accepted me in their midst, cold noses nuzzling my face and neck in the warm darkness, their sweet breath redolent of hay. I could see the vicarage in the distance, etched against the grey night in charcoal. My eyes followed the line of the hedge but I could see nothing. Suddenly something scraped across the slates on the roof, a movement too positive to be caused by the wind. Then another sound, a deliberate shifting of weight.

CHAPTER FOURTEEN

If a man can be said to tiptoe in inch-thick dung it is
what I did. I was moving towards the unglazed window
behind the manger. It was no more than a hole in the
wall through which bales of hay were tipped. I stood on
the manger and crawled through the hole, landing on
grass. There were a couple of plastic panniers at the
bottom of the fieldstone wall, inches away from my outstretched hand. I pressed the top of the nearer pannier,
feeling the compact firmness of the paper money packed
inside.

The noise on the roof was repeated. I crawled sideways towards the jetty and looked up at the soles of
two shoes. The Ratcatcher was lying flat on his
stomach, facing the fields, what looked like a sniper's
rifle resting on the ridge of the roof. His line of fire
took in the approach along the bank of the creek and
the path along the hedge. With a telescopic lens he
could pick off the six men creeping up on him, one
after another.

My first thought was for Jerry. If it hadn't been for
me he'd have been at home with his stamps. I crawled
back to the wall and pushed my arm through the hay-
hatch. The feed in the manger was old and dry. I
snapped my lighter. The manger was ablaze within
seconds. The bullocks charged out of the shed, their

bellowing echoing across the fields. I picked up a brick as the Ratcatcher slithered down from the roof, feet first. I caught him as he had caught me, just above the left ear. The rifle fell from his hands but not before I saw the look of recognition in his eyes. It was all I needed, that and to make a telephone call.

He was out but I held the rifle-barrel against his throat, shouting my head off till the rest of them came running. Mallory was first, taking the rifle from me. Someone held a flash on it. Mallory shook his head.

'Infra-red night-sights and an image-intensifier. Jesus *Christ*, what a bastard!'

He wiped the dung from his boots on a tussock of grass. Jerry had the panniers slung around his shoulders like a water-carrier. The Ratcatcher came to his senses and moved sideways, all in one, the movement of a snake disturbed in its sleep. Mallory grabbed him happily, throttling him in the crook of an elbow. Someone put the cuffs on him, others were stamping out the fire in the cattleshed. Jerry and I walked across the fields in silence. He dumped the panniers in the back of the Jaguar. It was somehow typical of him that he didn't even open them. I did it for him. The money was still in its original containers, plastic envelopes overprinted with the bank's Saluki motif.

I fastened the straps again. 'Haven't you *ever* been tempted, Jerry? Not *once* in the whole of your thirty-nine or whatever it is years?'

He grinned cheerfully. 'You mean the days of wine and roses – no. But I know you have.'

I lit a cigarette, surprised to find my hand perfectly steady.

'By what?'

188

He treasured the last of his smile and his eyes were friendly.

'What did you expect me to say – money? Hell no. Love, John. You're the last of the great romantics and no matter how bitter you think you feel, you'll fall again and again, once you're hungry enough. You need to be loved, John.'

We were silent again as the others came from the shrubbery, the Ratcatcher between burly-shouldered plain clothes men. He was scuffing his feet, hands manacled behind his back, carrying the prospect of endless years in a prison cell. He lifted his head as he passed the Jaguar, looking me full in the face and giving his harelipped sneer. They shoved him into the other car.

I was sitting in front. Mallory climbed into the driver's seat beside me. He collected Jerry's gun and put it in the glove-compartment together with his own. The others had taken the Ratcatcher's rifle. Mallory pulled his trousers out of his socks and straightened up.

'Did you check the gear, Jerry?'

Soo took his neatly-shod feet off the panniers. 'John looked at it. It'll be there.'

Mallory rubbed at a ginger eyebrow, searching for the right way of saying what he had to say.

'Thanks, Raven. I owe you one. It just could have been heavy for someone.'

It was after three by the clock on the dash. Across the green the silent houses slept on, the people inside probably dreaming of fields and spring. Me, I wanted to be in my home, in a hot bath with the record-player going.

'Well that's it,' said Mallory. 'This is going to mean

another session in court for you, Raven. You'll have to start charging appearance-money.'

I stretched, forgotten muscles creaking under the strain.

'You know what they say, "virtue's its own reward". Watch for "Window On The World".'

A yawn followed the stretch. I could call Noel Armstrong at the studio in the morning and set things up. But there was something else that came first.

'There's something you could do for me,' I said.

Old habits die hard and he was naturally suspicious. 'What do you want?' he asked guardedly.

I nodded at the radiophone. 'Do you mind if I call Drake?'

For a moment he looked puzzled then he started to laugh from his stomach, shivering a little at the end of each bellow. It was over as suddenly and he wiped his eyes.

'Help yourself,' he said with a sweeping gesture.

The number was etched on my brain. I could see the mock-tudor house, the shingle on the gate, the flagged pathway through bullied rosebushes. I picked up the phone and went through Mobile. It was some time before the number answered, the voice sleepy and belligerent.

'Yes?'

'Commander Drake?'

'Yes. Who is this?'

'Digby O'Dell, your friendly undertaker.'

I could hear a clock ticking then he must have covered the mouthpiece with his hand. He was back again, warning me.

'Raven? Now listen to me, Raven...'

'Listen to *me*,' I said. 'Power corrupts. There are things going on that you ought to know about.'

I could hear a woman's voice, shrill and defensive. It had to be his wife, he could never have had a lover.

'Commander?' I said.

'I'm having this call traced,' he said tightly. 'You're going to be in trouble.'

'I doubt it.' The other two in the car were straining to hear every word.

'The Flying Squad's covered itself with glory. Inspector Mallory has captured himself a top villain, thanks to you know who. I thought that you should be the first to know, Commander.'

His breathing was heavy. 'You're mad, you bastard. And don't think I've finished with you.'

'Ah, but you have,' I said. 'You see, life gets tougher, old buddy. Sleep tight.'

I put the phone back on its rest. 'London, officer, and no rash driving.'

Mallory switched on the motor. 'You realise that bastard's going to have a go at me.'

'A tinkling cymbal,' I said. 'Unnoticed in the triumphant blare of trumpets.'

'Goddammit, you *are* mad,' he decided. 'As mad as a hatter.' He looked at the phone, shaking his head. 'What the fuck was all *that* about?'

'What did you expect me to say to him?' I asked. 'Goodnight, sweetheart?'

He flashed the headlamps, indicating that the other car should follow.

'Well, as long as it gives you satisfaction ...'

'And it does,' I said. A great weight had lifted from my shoulders.

He tipped his hat back, locked his hands on the wheel and concentrated on manoeuvring through the vicarage gates. But he couldn't let it alone.

'Nutty as a fruitcake and dangerous with it.'

'Wrong again,' I corrected. 'I'm the last of the great romantics.'

I closed my eyes but not before I saw the look on Jerry's face.